RESIST AND EVADE

Book Two in the *Blue Lives Apocalypse* Series

A novel by Lee West

First edition.

Copyright Information

To the brave men and women in blue—who proudly serve our communities.

And to my family, for their never-ending love and support.

Prologue

Officer Price walked toward the communications "shed," trying to shake the sleep from his foggy head. When the police force left the Evansville PD headquarters, the chief had insisted that they disassemble most of the communications system so they could reassemble it when they relocated to the new HQ. The chief hoped it would give them a link to the outside world, in addition to providing a way to communicate with any mobile patrols they started sending on reconnaissance missions into the surrounding communities.

Upon arriving at the new HQ, Price didn't think it possible to get the communications rig up and running. The place was a summer camp for rich kids, not exactly an ideal replacement for the Evansville Police Department's headquarters. Fortunately, they had arrived during the camp's weekly turnover. The place was half empty, except for the kids who stayed all summer and the camp counselors. They had no idea anything had happened outside the camp until the police showed up and started moving in.

Initially, the counselors were skeptical of the chief's explanation—until the parents started to arrive. Wave after wave of them, mostly on foot, showed up every day to claim their kids. It became so common that the kids waited around to see who would be claimed next in a joyful, tearful reunion. Although they tried not to show it, the few kids whose parents had not yet arrived appeared more and more tense as the days continued, and it became clear that nobody would likely arrive to meet them. Many of the remaining kids lived a full day's drive or long plane ride from the camp. They'd more or less given up hope after a week passed with no word from their parents.

Much to Price's surprise, they were able to reassemble the communications system at the camp. They used a generator and typically ran the system late at night, during the agreed upon communication period. Tonight was no different for Price. He would make a pot of strong coffee and try not to feel like an eavesdropper as he listened to Marta and Doris chat. The two women appeared to have become good friends. Although their conversations were quick, he could tell they both cherished the time spent together. Not hard to imagine given the solitude of their circumstances. Their talks reminded him of his mother and aunt sitting around the kitchen table, chatting the night away over a bottle of merlot.

Settled in the shed, he brewed his coffee and turned on the radio. None of the Evansville PD's radio monitors ever let either Doris or Marta know that they listened to the conversations. For security purposes, the chief thought, for now it would be better if few knew they had a functional radio. Night after night, one of the officers waited for the two women to chat. Night after night, it was the same sort of conversation—snippets about their lives and their hopes for the future. The officers could clearly hear Doris's side of the conversation, since she was closer, but Marta's voice was often obscured by static. The distance between Marta's radio and the HQ's receiver proved to be too great for reliable, clear transmissions.

Leaning back in his chair, Officer Price sipped his coffee and tuned the system. Sharp crackles punctuated the quiet night, indicating that someone was talking. Price adjusted the system a little more, trying to clear the static. Marta's voice broke through the white noise.

"Hello? Doris, come in!" screamed Marta.

Hearing the panic in Marta's voice, Price leaned in, listening intently.

"Doris! Come in, PLEASE!"

A short pause ensued before a different voice crackled.

"Marta, it's Doris. Are you okay? Over."

Static and high-pitched "squawks" were the only reply. Price again tried to adjust the radio, but his efforts seemed to make the white noise grow louder. *Shit!* If he didn't get this right in the next few seconds, he could possibly lose them entirely. Furiously manipulating the controls, Doris's voice became clear again.

"Holy—uh, I mean copy that. How long do I have? It's after midnight. I can't leave in the pitch dark. What should I do?"

How long until what? Static answered his question.

"Okay. I can do that. I think I know where to go," said Doris. "I'll leave a little before first light."

Price quickly put together what had just occurred. The New Order must have discovered the location of Doris's house, which had served as the second safe house on the trail used by the police to flee Porter for the safety of the HQ. The New Order, as they now called themselves, consisted of a gang of escaped prisoners from the local PrisCorp prison facility, who hunted down and viciously killed all law enforcement personnel. They needed to help Doris, fast. If the New Order found her, she would be killed for her role in assisting the cops.

Crap!

Price quickly stood up, knocking over his chair with a loud bang. With his flashlight in hand, he ran through the dark forest to the chief's cabin. Knocking rapidly on the cabin door, Price yelled in a shaky voice for the chief.

"Chief, it's Price. You need to wake up. We have a situation."

The chief's strong, tall body filled the doorframe. He rubbed his eyes and yawned with an exaggerated sigh. "Slow down and tell me what happened."

"I was monitoring radio chatter and think I just heard Marta telling Doris to flee her home. From what I could tell, Doris is leaving at first light. I have no idea where she intends to go or what she will leave behind for the New Order men to discover. She sounded terrified. Doris may or may not know the location of Scott Marsh's house, the third safe house."

"Alright. Nice work. Wake up the others. We need to assemble an assault team immediately. We don't have a minute to spare."

Price ran to the center of the camp, where the dinner bell hung from the eve of the large wraparound farmer's porch. The camp must have used the bell to signify the beginning or the end of activities. When the police first moved to the camp, they designated the bell as their low-tech emergency communications system. Instead of a group text to the entire force, they would now ring the bell to warn of an attack.

With a shaky hand, Price pulled the bell's cord over and over again, the bell's urgent metal clang echoing through the sleeping camp.

Chapter One

Doris walked swiftly and deliberately through the forest. It had been a long time since she'd hiked on a rough trail. Finding her footing in the predawn hours' darkness proved to be a greater challenge than she expected. She began to wonder if leaving a little later might have been a better idea, since she really did not seem to be making much headway.

Marta's grave warning that the New Order had discovered her house terrified Doris. Up until that transmission, Doris believed what others told her about the situation in the world, but never truly thought she would be affected by it. She figured as long as she welcomed the escaping cops or "runners," giving them safe haven for a day while they worked their way to the HQ, she would be fine—not really part of what happened.

Now she was literally running for her life. If the New Order men found her, they would kill her on the spot. She had no doubt about that. She always knew the aid she gave the police put her in a particularly dangerous position, but helping the police was the only thing she could think to do in the circumstances. Besides, she knew her son, a fallen Marine, would have done the same thing, without hesitation. It had been the right thing to do, and she'd do it again given the chance.

The trail grew thicker and wilder as she walked, leading Doris to believe she'd somehow lost the main path and had veered off into the forest. Stopping, she dropped her pack and fished out the map she'd barely remembered to bring. Looking around the forest and listening for anyone near her, she chanced using her flashlight. She laid the map and compass as flat as she could on the ground, not sure she could make any sense of the two right now. The times she and her son had gone hiking, they merely walked along well-marked trails. This was something different entirely. Her heart sank as she started to wonder if she did, in fact, go far off the trail, losing her way in the darkness. A navigational error could lead her into New Order territory or cause her to be hopelessly lost in the forest, with little by way of supplies or anticipated assistance. She might be better off staying put until it was daylight.

As she sat studying the map and compass, an unusual sound caught her attention. The sound definitely did not belong to the forest. It had a metallic quality to it. The sound grew louder, approaching her from the south. Or was it the north? She had no idea. Panic washed over her as she lay flat against the ground, trying desperately to conceal her location from whatever approached.

Small moving lights appeared in the shadowy recesses of the forest. *Damn it! They're moving right toward me! Shit!*

Doris knew she could not move without risking detection, so she tried as best she could to remain flat and calm. Just as she was about to break cover and run away, a line of bicycles silently streamed past her location. The light from their headlamps gave her a glimpse of the riders. The first thing she noticed was that they were heavily armed, each with a rifle slung over his or her shoulders. A few wore cargo shorts, but most wore long pants. They all sported tactical vests, which she guessed had been outfitted with body armor plates. She knew that from what her son had told her. She also knew the plates were heavy. It wasn't until the second-to-last rider passed that she saw EVANSVILLE PD displayed on the back of one of the vests.

The police? Here? Why? Where are they going?

Standing up from the ground on her creaky legs, she thought about calling out to them, but they'd already disappeared down the trail. She gathered her gear and walked toward the trail, hoping to run into another group of police officers. Doris found the trail again and waited, a few quiet minutes passing before she decided to continue on her own. She felt better about the entire situation, knowing the police were on the trail and had probably cleared it of New Order riffraff.

Doris walked for another minute or two, paying close attention to where she put her feet on the uneven trail. She never saw the man that stepped onto the trail ahead of her until she had nearly bumbled into his rifle barrel.

"Hands up where we can see them!" said the man.

We?

Figures appeared on both sides of the trail, wordlessly, quickly and efficiently enveloping her with their guns drawn. Doris dropped her pack and slowly raised her trembling hands toward the sky.

"State your name!"

"Doris Venture," she said.

The man lowered his weapon. "Stand down! Stand down! She's our package."

At once, the men and women quickly stood at ease with their weapons pointed at the ground.

"Good morning, Ms. Venture. I'm Officer Price from the Grant Police Department. Sorry for the drama, but we can never be too careful."

Doris accepted Officer Price's outstretched hand.

"Officer Price? Where're you all heading? I thought the HQ was north of here. I'm trying to get there myself. Geez—I must've really gotten lost."

"Nope—you're good. We're heading south to your house to push back against any attack the New Order might have planned."

One of the other officers stepped onto the trail, next to Officer Price.

"Good morning, ma'am. I'm Officer Jensen," he said. "I'm in charge of the foot mobile group."

Doris shook the man's thick, sweaty hand, still feeling confused. She had no idea that her and Marta's conversations were being monitored or that the police cared to defend her home. Why would they?

"Price, will you escort Ms. Venture to the next safe house. Then you can come back to join us."

"Yes, sir. Ms. Venture, do you need a minute to rest, or are you travel ready?"

"I'm okay to keep moving, but I won't be running," she said.

"No problem, ma'am, we'll keep it to whatever pace you need. You've been a valuable asset to the police during this crisis. You're somewhat of a legend in our circles. There's no way the chief will let anything happen to you or your home."

A small blush crossed Doris's face as she rubbed a tear from her eye. Touched by the care shown to her, all she could respond with was a simple, "Thank you." Through a series of silent commands, Officer Jensen reformed the group. The police ran silently and bravely into harm's way. Doris lingered for a moment, recalling memories of her deceased son. She knew he would have joined this courageous group of men and women in the defense of their home. A proud nostalgia warmed her spirits.

"Ma'am? You ready?"

"I sure am."

Chapter Two

Sam Archer moved through the storage unit as quietly as possible to avoid waking Jane or Lea. The three of them had hidden in the storage locker since they'd rescued Lea from her ex-boyfriend Tank. Lea had been home alone when the lights went out because Sam and Jane had been on a backcountry-hiking trip in the nearby mountains. They had rushed back as quickly as possible through New Order–controlled territory. Their trek had been perilous from the start. The things they'd witnessed were beyond Sam's ability to make sense of.

"Good morning, handsome," whispered Jane, in a sleepy voice.

"Good morning, beautiful."

"Or is it afternoon? Being inside a closed storage unit is a little disorientating."

Sam chuckled. "Yeah, almost like being in a casino—you have no idea how long you've been there or what time it is. The next time I plan for a disaster, I'll try to get a storage unit with a skylight, just for you."

Jane stretched her petite, slim body luxuriously across the camp cot, like an agile cat rousing from an afternoon nap in the sun. Sam admired her ability to sleep and look completely comfortable in almost any situation. It was one of the many things he loved about his wife of twenty-five years.

Although the unit was large and served their survival needs well, it did not offer much by way of privacy, especially in their makeshift bathroom. A shower curtain suspended from the ceiling created a tiny nook around their "toilet." However, the shower curtain did nothing to shield the community space from the sounds and smells made by the bathroom's occupant. Coming out of the bathroom, Jane washed her hands in a sudsy basin placed next to the bathroom.

"I think that thing will need to be emptied soon."

"Okay—I'll get it later today."

The bucket worked great but needed to be kept clean, especially in tight quarters. He was surprised how quickly it had filled up.

Her daughter poked her head out of the top of her blanket.

"I'm starving," she said.

"May I interest you in a granola bar and dried apples? Maybe go easy on your stomach at first."

"Sounds great, Dad," said Lea, with a smile.

"How are you feeling, sweetie?" asked Jane.

"Better. A lot better—I'm not achy all over and feel like my energy is coming back," said Lea.

"You went through quite an ordeal. I'm not sure what was more of a shock on your system, the dehydration, starvation or Tank's fists," said Jane.

Lea seemed to tense at Tank's name. Sam needed to quickly shift the conversation.

"Okay—if you're feeling ready, I think we should consider leaving the unit either late tonight or early in the morning. We could get the bikes and carriers ready now," said Sam.

"I think tomorrow morning would be best. We can all use another solid night of sleep. Plus, we can really take some time planning our route and supplies. We obviously can't bring everything," said Jane.

"No. We can't take everything. We'll need to bring just the essentials," said Sam.

"Maybe we need to ditch the idea of using the bike carriers?"

Turning to Lea, Sam found himself once again admiring Lea's ability to quickly grasp the situation and add to the conversation.

"I agree. Let's plan to take just the saddlebags and backpacks. Then, once we figure out where we're going, we can always come back for more," said Sam.

"Sounds like a plan—I'll start loading the packs. Where do you want to go? The cottages up north? The HQ? Or to Scott Marsh's house?" asked Jane.

"Didn't Charlie and Mark go to that guy Scott's house?"

"Yeah. They might still be there if we get there tomorrow. I know they planned to stay for at least a couple of days before heading to HQ. Maybe that's our best bet. If we ultimately want to join everyone at HQ, it would be nice to walk the trail with Charlie and Mark."

"Yeah, those two rock. I felt really safe with them around," said Lea.

"I think we all did," replied Sam.

Sam pulled out a map and settled down next to Jane at the camp table. The map, like them, had been through a lot and showed its wear. When Charlie had told Sam and Jane about the location of the safe house, he did not mark the map. They wanted to be sure there was no written record of its location just in case the New Order got a hold of the map. Finding one safe house would quickly lead them to the next one and, ultimately, the HQ. Sam concentrated to remember exactly where Scott's house sat on the map.

"It's here," said Jane with a jab of her finger at the map.

"You sure? I thought it was a little this way," said Sam, sliding his finger east on the map.

"No, I'm sure. I remember thinking their house must be really serene, surrounded by the forest and mountains. It just sort of stuck in my mind."

"Okay. That makes sense. I think Charlie said he managed to get to our house from there in about four hours. So you're probably right."

"A four-hour ride on a loaded-down bike while carrying a heavy pack? Oh brother. Wake me up when it's over," said Lea.

"Funny, I was thinking the same thing." Jane smiled as she leaned in to squeeze Lea's hand.

Chapter Three

Charlie dozed in, but mostly out of sleep. Scott and Barbara Marsh had a nice house, but it was not exactly set up for more than a couple of visitors at a time. Charlie insisted that Mark take the spare room for the night, while he slept on the sofa. Like most sofas, it offered perfect comfort for watching television and napping, but try to get a good night's sleep and the piece of furniture morphed into a backbreaker.

Charlie was exhausted from the previous night's battle with the New Order thugs that had kidnapped the Archers' daughter. He'd been on the move nonstop for the past few days. After the shoot-out, the group had made its way to the Archers' survival storage unit. Charlie felt bad leaving the Archers right away; however, he knew if he did not make it back to the Marshes' house that evening, Mike Sparr, a Porter police officer, might try to rescue him. Adding Mike Sparr to the already dangerous equation was not something Charlie wanted to risk.

Sam had loaded Charlie's and Mark's packs with enough dried food and water to resupply the Marshes for at least a week, with rationing. Barbara Marsh burst into tears at the sight of the food. Scott, a man who tended to be more proud than practical, merely nodded his head, unsure if he should take what likely seemed like a handout. Jenny Sparr, Mike's young daughter, had no such hesitations accepting the food. From the living room sofa, Charlie could hear Jenny's excited voice.

"Wow! Dried bananas!" she exclaimed.

"Slow down, honey. We can only have a little nibble right now. Besides, this is Mr. and Mrs. Marsh's food. We need to be sure they have plenty when we leave," said Mike.

Rubbing his stubbled face and walking into the kitchen, Charlie noticed that the pile of food remained where he'd put it last night. The Marshes had not touched it.

"You guys are up early," said Charlie.

"Not really—you're up late—its 10:00 a.m. You were out cold for hours. We just didn't want to wake you," said Mike.

"You snore louder than Daddy does," said Mike's daughter.

"Jenny! Sorry, man. But yeah—you were snoring up a storm."

"It was a rough night," said Charlie, with a solemn glance to the ground.

"Did everything turn out alright for the Archers?"

Charlie knew Mike needed to be careful about what Jenny heard.

"Yes. Everything is great with them. Their daughter, Lea, is fine. They decided to rest there a few days and then they might meet us at HQ. When we left, they were not too sure where they'd go."

"Speaking of HQ—when do you want to get out of here? If you need a little time to recuperate, no worries. We can hang here a little longer, especially with this amazing load of food. Was all of this from the Archers?"

"Yes. They have a nice setup. They're also very generous people. Given the current situation, many people would be stingy with their supplies, for good reason. Have you seen Mark?"

"He made his way through here about thirty minutes ago. He went out for a jog or a walk. I'm not too sure. He said he needed to get a handle on his surroundings and then just walked out. Who is he?"

"Mark is one of Jane and Sam's neighbors. He's also a former

Force Recon Marine. Probably one of the most accurate snipers I've ever seen. Last night could have been a lot different without him."

"What's a sniper?"

Charlie shot Mike an apologetic look.

"Just someone who likes to be accurate with things—you know, someone who does a really good job when they're working on something. So you want more dried apple?"

Charlie could not help but smile at Mark's use of food to distract Jenny. Anytime an uncomfortable situation arose in his own home when he was a child, his mother would pull out snacks. Although Charlie had no children, he started to understand the seemingly universal use of food to bribe and quiet them. Probably not that different with grown men under normal circumstances.

The screen door closed with a loud bang as Mark walked into the house. Both Charlie and Mike tensed at the sound, unsure of the house's rhythms.

"Hey, guys. This place is amazing. I took a walk around the perimeter. It's a beautiful location," said Mark.

"Thank you!" said Barbara, walking into the kitchen.

Charlie noticed the sideways glance Barbara gave the food. Every time he came to the Marshes' house, they looked increasingly worse, especially Barbara. Barbara's already slim frame could not withstand the severe caloric deprivation forced upon it. Her eyes were sunken into their sockets and rimmed in black. Charlie suspected that Scott's ego stood in the way of Barbara and the food given to them by the Archers. Scott, on the other hand, fared better. Although Scott looked as unkempt as everyone, Charlie did not notice much of a reduction in the size of Scott's rotund abdomen.

"Barbara, we'll leave you our water so you guys can cook the grains," said Charlie.

"We won't be needing anything. You can go ahead and take all this stuff with you when you leave. The Marshes do not accept handouts," said Scott, walking into the room.

Mark shared a tense, knowing look with Charlie. Something was wrong with Scott.

"We're planning to leave later today. The HQ is only about five hours from here. We should be able to get there before dinner. Getting there before nightfall will allow the sentries to recognize us. We don't want to be misidentified. You both should come with us," said Charlie to Scott and Barbara. "There's only one more officer in Porter that needs to be moved out. The situation has changed dramatically, preventing us from getting to that person—whoever it is. At this point, there really isn't the need for a third safe house. You would be much better off coming with us than staying here on your own."

"Besides, you're a great carpenter, Scott. The HQ could really use your skills. From what I heard, they need all the help they can get," said Mark.

A glimmer of pride shone in Scott's eyes. The thought of being useful again seemed to really appeal to him. Charlie silently admired Mark's ability to steer Scott into making the right decision.

"Well, so long as you think we'd be helping. I don't want to be a burden on anyone."

"You'd be invaluable."

An almost imperceptible smile grew on Barbara's face.

"Okay. It's decided. When do you want to leave?" asked Mike.

"How about an hour. That'll give us plenty of time to repack and organize for the trip," said Charlie.

"I better get busy if we're leaving that soon," said Barbara as she buzzed out of the room.

"Us too. Come on, Jenny, let's get our things together," said Mike.

~ ~ ~

Charlie sat alone with his thoughts on the front porch while the others packed. It had been two weeks since he'd seen Gayle. Gayle

Jones was an officer in the Porter Police Department. She lived in the Porter city center. They had been together for two years, prompting Charlie to buy a house near town. He would do anything to be near her now—and for the rest of their lives. He had planned to propose to her on an upcoming vacation to the Florida panhandle. Unfortunately, the lights went out two weeks before their trip.

When everything started to fall apart in Porter, she was one of the first people he moved out of town. He knew she would never be safe with the New Order around. He also knew that his judgment would be clouded with her in the thick of things. He would naturally act to protect her, even to his own peril. Getting Gayle to HQ early in the game was a way for him to keep her safe, and function effectively as the first point of contact for police officers smuggled out of town. Gayle was less than excited to be sent into "exile," as she put it. He knew she wanted to stay and help him, but there was no way he could do his job protecting the other officers with her around. On top of that, two of them sneaking through the woods doubled their chances of getting caught.

Seeing Gayle again was on the top of Charlie's list for wanting to leave the Marshes' house today. The sooner he confirmed she was safe, the better he would feel. He knew all too well that things could go really wrong along the trail to the HQ. Nothing but holding her in his arms would reassure him.

"You expecting company?" asked Mark, from the shadowy recesses of the house.

"Nope," said Charlie, trying to remain calm.

Charlie knew unexpected company could only mean one thing—the New Order had found Scott's house.

"We have unidentified contacts inbound to your two o'clock."

"Roger that."

Charlie slowly and casually stood from the porch step, stretching and scanning the surrounding area. In his peripheral vision, he detected movement in the dense bushes lining the horse trail. The trail extended from Porter, past Doris's house, eventually snaking to Scott's house and beyond. He needed to get inside fast. Grabbing his pack, he slowly moved inside and shut the door while trying to remain as nonchalant as possible. Giving the enemy any indication they had been spotted could destroy the advantage Mark's keen observation afforded them.

"Mike is spotting them through the upstairs window. I need to get around back to see if we're being surrounded," stated Mark as he moved quickly through the house.

"Where are Jenny and the Marshes?"

"Basement."

Charlie quickly moved the sofa in front of the living room window. Settling in behind the couch, he scanned the trail and surrounding woods. A man's torso appeared in the distance. Charlie did not recognize the man. Then another head appeared, bobbing in and out of view behind the first man. He could swear the second person was a woman. The crack of a gunshot rang out through the house, breaking the silence. *Shit. Mike is shooting. What the hell?*

The bullet must have missed, since the two people remained in the open. They seemed dazed at the sudden shock of being shot at, as though they weren't sure what happened. A second bullet ricocheted off the tree next to the first man, who dove to the ground out of Charlie's view. The second figure remained frozen long enough for him to get a good look. Doris. *Fuck!*

"STOP SHOOTING! STAND DOWN! Possible friendlies!"

"Back is clear. Did you say they're friendlies?" asked Mark, running back into the living room.

"It's Doris and some guy. Damn it. Why the fuck is he shooting before we identified them?"

Mike came running down the stairs to join them.

"You know them?" he asked.

"Yes. It's Doris and some guy. We need to be certain it's just them and not some sort of trick. Mike, go back upstairs, but hold your fire.

Mark, you watch our backs for an ambush. Doris wasn't supposed to be moving to this location. Look sharp. But don't shoot until I say so."

The men quickly disbursed. Charlie moved back to the window and viewed the area. No movement. If it was Doris and a friend, they were probably glued to the ground, terrified that they would get shot. If not, they might be recalibrating their attack—using Doris as bait. *Shit*. This was not good. Scratching his head, Charlie scrambled for a plan that wouldn't get them all killed.

"Identify yourselves!" he shouted.

No sound.

"Identify yourselves or we start shooting again!"

Rustling in the bushes. Then the man's voice rang out.

"Officer Price with the Grant PD. I have Doris Venture with me."

Grant PD?

"Stand up slowly, hands in the air."

Officer Price and Doris stood very hesitantly, unsure if they would be shot where they stood.

"Move toward the house very slowly."

The two emerged from the trail. Charlie could now clearly see them and their immediately surrounding areas.

"Drop your weapon!"

Officer Price slowly removed his pistol from its holster and tossed it in the grass.

"Doris, why're you here!" shouted Charlie.

He'd never met Officer Price and had no reason to think the Grant Police Department worked in this area or to believe the man was in fact "Officer Price."

"Last night, I got a warning from Marta that the New Order was coming up the trail! Officer Price and the others found me heading here!" she shouted with an unsteady voice.

"Stand down! Stand down! They're friendly!"

Charlie ran out the front door to greet them.

"Holy crap! Sorry for the reception. We had no idea you were on your way here or that anything had happened."

"A few of us from the Grant PD were at the HQ when we overheard the call from Marta to Doris."

"Overheard? How can you guys hear anything that far north?"

"The antenna at Doris's house could send a transmission to the moon. We're able to hear her loud and clear, but not always the Porter radio. Last night, we heard enough to get our asses down here pronto. The chief wants to keep that radio operational."

"Did you say you're from Grant?" asked Mark.

"Yeah. We caught wind of the HQ being formed and made our way up there. We can fill you guys in on the details later. Right now, I need to drop her off and head back to Doris's house. The team plans on ambushing whatever the New Order sends down the trail."

The others joined the group on the lawn. Scott and Barbara held each other while Mike tried to comfort Jenny.

"Sorry about the shot over your heads. That was my bad. Just a little overanxious given the situation," said Mike.

"I'm with you. We had no real way to let you know we were coming."

"Alright. New plan. I need to go with Officer Price," Charlie started saying.

"Please call me Joe."

"Okay. I need to go with Joe to Doris's house. Mike, you'll have to take the route to HQ yourself. Can you manage?" asked Charlie.

Mike hesitated long enough for Charlie to realize that he did not feel confident about getting safely to HQ.

"I'll go with Joe and then rejoin you guys at HQ. That way you can get them to HQ and Joe has some backup," said Mark.

Considering Mark's offer for a moment, Charlie said, "Mark is a former Marine Force Recon, and probably one of the best snipers I have ever seen. He can more than handle it."

"Fine. But we can't offer you a weapon. Supplies are very thin."

"Don't worry about me. I have that covered," said Mark, with a slight smile.

Chapter Four

Brown sat in the communications center of the Porter Police Department, considering his situation. Brown had joined the New Order group mostly to survive the harsh new reality that had descended on the land. Knowing that he had no ready contacts in the area, he rightly estimated that getting food and other necessities would not be possible on his own. Siding with the New Order was the logical move at first; however, the Boss had become more and more unstable as time passed. He was making irrational decisions, which would eventually get them all killed. His best bet was to help the police at this point and secure his safety in the long run.

He'd aided the cops by giving them advance warning of New Order's plans. Once the Boss discovered the horse trail, Brown realized it would only be a matter of time before they would find that lady Doris and her house. Although Marta wouldn't admit it, he knew the cops had created an underground railroad to remove their own from Porter. Doris would be killed on the spot or tortured for information and fun, whichever the Boss was in the mood for. He hoped Doris had already hit the trail.

The Boss had roughly thirty of his "soldiers" headed in her direction. Some were running the trail while the others drove the rough terrain. The drivers needed the guys on the trail to keep them following the route. Brown knew that the process of guiding the drivers from the trail would slow them down considerably. All the men were heavily armed, with the weapons stolen either from the Porter Police Department or houses they raided. The door to the communications room swung open with a loud bang.

"What the fuck are you still doing here?" shouted the Boss. "All you motherfuckers are supposed to be on that trail."

"I assumed you wanted me here monitoring radio traffic."

There was no way Brown was running that trail with the rest of the idiots. He'd managed to slip away back to the communications room when the Boss was busy shouting orders at the men.

"Monitoring? Is that what you call it? I call it ain't doing shit. You haven't heard a damn thing since you started."

"No. But it could be that no one else has the generators we do to run their radios," offered Brown.

The Boss eyed him suspiciously as he walked closer to Brown.

Jabbing his finger into Brown's shoulder, the Boss said, "You better start hearing something, hoss, or your fucking days as a shitball radio jockey are over. You get me?"

"I'll try harder. There has to be someone on the radio somewhere."

The Boss lingered for another moment, staring intensely at Brown. The Boss had a way of looking through people. It was his favorite intimidation method. Hell, it worked every time on Brown. Beads of sweat slowly trickled down Brown's back. Finally, the Boss broke his stare.

"I'll be watching you."

Alone again in the communications room, Brown knew he could not last much longer in this position before he got himself killed. He secretly wished the cops would hurry up and push into town.

"Hey, Brown. Give me a hand in the supply room," whispered Johnny.

"What the hell? Why?"

"I need you to watch out for me. My grandma needs more food. I figured while they're out, I would stock her up."

"Shit. You're going to get us both killed," said Brown. "Come on, I'll help you, but let's make it fast."

The two moved quickly through the quiet station. The interior spaces of the station were dark and shadowy from the lack of light. Even when the sun sat high in the sky, the station seemed to have a gloom that could not be chased away.

"I'm gonna grab some cans and other shit for her," said Johnny. "What do you think they're going to find on the trail?"

"Don't know. Nothing, I guess."

"You're probably right. Glad I didn't have to go. I guess being the Boss's personal shit doer has its advantages."

"Yeah, I guess."

The Boss's booming voice could be heard from down the hall.

"Johnny! Johnny! Where the fuck you at?" said the Boss.

"Damn it. I need to get out there. Grab this bag and hide it for me. I'll get it from you later!" said Johnny, running from the room.

"Shit, man. Are you fucking kidding me?" said Brown, holding the bag away from him like it was radioactive.

"I'll meet you in the comms room later," said Johnny.

Johnny jogged down the hall toward the Boss's office. Getting caught trying to steel food would get Brown killed. The Boss did not take stealing lightly. He quickly stashed the small bag of cans under the radio console, examining the hiding place from several locations in the room. Satisfied that their deception would remain undetected, he started to relax.

"New roommate, shitball!" The Boss's loud voice rang out behind him.

Straightening up from a crouched position, Brown could not be entirely certain the Boss or the guy standing with him didn't see him hiding the bag.

"This here is Bet. He's gonna be joining you, helping you listen and shit."

"Hey," said Bet unenthusiastically.

"Really, Boss, I got this. I don't need the help."

"You ain't heard shit. You're getting the help."

Bet settled into the chair beside Brown. If Bet heard Marta's transmissions or any other ones, the Boss would quickly figure out he had been lying all along about not hearing anything on the radio. He needed to act fast.

"Why the fuck do they call you Bet?"

"I can burp the entire alphabet—bet is short for alphabet."

"Nice."

Purposely knocking his drink over, Brown yelled, "Oh shit! Go grab me some napkins, man!"

Bet ran out of the room. During his absence, Brown quickly reached over and disabled the antenna from the system. No one would notice unless they knew what to look for. The guy returned a few seconds later with a roll of paper towels.

"Thanks, man," said Brown, mopping up the spilled warm Mountain Dew.

Chapter Five

Tank pounded his way through the Archers' house, determined to figure out where they had fled after their escape. Fury had overtaken him last night when he realized that he could not grab that dumb bitch Lea without possibly getting killed. Her bitch mother, a stupid cop on top of it all, must have gotten a couple other cops to help with Lea's rescue. Otherwise, they would have been no match for Tank and his guys.

Now he had to deal with the humiliation of his crew knowing that dumb bitch had escaped his grasp and killed a tidy number of his people in the process. A sign of weakness this big could mean the difference between Tank advancing in the New Order or getting killed by some punk-ass gangbanger looking to better his future. No. Tank would get that dumb bitch Lea and her mother. He had plans for the mother. She would be the prize catch. He planned to make her the centerpiece of the activities he had planned for Lea and her family. After that, Tank's place in the New Order would be solidified. No one would step up to him ever again. Not unless they wanted their head mounted to a street sign.

Moving through the Archers' house, the stench of Chill's body overwhelmed him. The dude stank bad enough when he was alive. Tank replayed the entire scene in his head again. The Archers had been outside shooting at his men, but Tank rightly realized they would not risk shooting their own daughter. The bullets stopped the moment he walked out with that dumb bitch. He stuffed her in one of the trucks they had and simply drove off. The only thing he didn't count on was that dumb bitch throwing herself from the truck as they sped out of the neighborhood.

Fucking bitch!

Reliving the events of the previous night reignited Tank's fury. Seeing Lea push open the door and roll out onto the pavement made his blood boil with murderous rage. No one dared to cross Tank. Not even that dumb bitch and her cop mom. He would find them both, and they would pay dearly.

Room by room, Tank searched for any sign of their whereabouts. Pulling out drawers, he dumped their contents on the floor, kicking through their belongings as though they were discarded trash. He ripped the place apart, becoming more and more enraged by the minute at his inability to find any sort of clue.

Standing in the kitchen near Chill's body, Tank stared at the pictures on the fridge. Magnets from various trips held the family's memories. The Grand Teton magnet held a picture of Lea graduating from high school. The Florida Sunshine State magnet held a picture of the three of them smiling over a table of food at a resort. Picture by picture the Archers mocked him with their happy, smiling faces.

"Where the FUCK are you!" growled Tank, his fists punching the wall next to the fridge.

On the side of the fridge, a lone business card hung silently by a "#1 Dad" magnet. Just a card. Nothing more. Nothing less. Tank saw the card through his peripheral vision. Grabbing it, Tank turned it over in his large dirty hands. On the back of the card someone had written #23C.

Bingo!

"Get your shit together. We're moving out!" yelled Tank to the other men searching the house.

He never would have thought of a storage unit. Why would he? Who would go to a storage unit?

"Where to? You find something?" yelled Salem as he ran downstairs.

"I found this."

Triumphantly, Tank held the card high for the men to see as though it were pure gold.

"What is it?"

"It's a card to that storage place on Michigan Road, with the number 23C written on the back!"

"Shit! You think that's where they're hiding?"

"How the fuck should I know? We check it out. We either find that dumb bitch or we find some shit we can use. Either way, we need to get the fuck out of this shithole. The smell is killing me."

Chapter Six

Jane crouched low in the shallow creek, swirling the water in and out of the red bucket. Since they didn't plan on staying at the storage unit long term, they'd decided to use a bucket for peeing instead of the compost unit. They'd also gone through a lot of water trying to rehydrate themselves, which filled the bucket quicker than they had expected. Sam had offered to clean it again, but Jane needed a break from the storage unit.

Living inside a closed storage unit presented its challenges, a lack of fresh air being one of them. Sam had done an excellent job stocking them with everything they needed for at least a year, and with rationing, they could likely go longer, but they'd probably go crazy long before they ran out of food. The locker unit had already shrunk inside her head, and they'd been there less than twenty-four hours. The trick would be finding another location to safely ride out the New Order storm.

Standing and stretching by the water's edge, Jane lingered. She had no real reason to rush back to the unit. Having a creek near the unit turned out to really benefit them. All part of Sam's master plan, if they decided to remain in place for a long period of time. There was only so much water you could store in the locker.

Jane surveyed the land beyond the creek. She realized for the first time how sparse the trail was in these woods. She hoped Charlie and

Mark made it back to Scott's house without incident. Getting lost and veering into the New Order was something that had almost happened to her and Sam. Time to get moving.

Jane scrambled up the embankment, careful not to get scratched up again in the tangles of underbrush that grew on the sloped terrain. As she approached the top of the incline, near the storage facility's fence, she heard voices. She lowered herself to the slimmest profile she could manage and unholstered her pistol. Two cars pulled up to the Store-Right facility fence, on the far side of the compound.

"Hey, Tank, it's over here—number 23C is on this side!" yelled an excited male voice.

They found us.

Jane's heart raced as she considered her options. Lea and Sam were in unit 52L. Sam had moved their things from 23C to 52L in order to get more space. He also liked that 52L sat in the back of the facility, near the woods. No one would see them coming and going from the road. Unit 23C was located on the other side of the facility, closer to the main road. Not far enough away to shield them entirely if someone happened to come in their direction. They needed to act fast.

"Get something to pry it open with!" shouted someone that sounded a lot like Tank.

Jane slipped through the fence and made her way to unit 52L. She lay flat on the ground and nudged the door open a foot or so, just enough to slide her slim figure under the door. Once through, she quietly shut the door, careful not to make a sound.

"Hey, honey, we can't remember—is Uno won by getting the most cards or points?" asked Sam, with a casual air.

Jane's eyes took a second to adjust to the gloomy interior of the unit. The battery-powered lanterns did a fair job of lighting the space, but it still seemed like a coffin after being outside.

"Ssh! Ssh! Quiet. They're out there. Tank and his men found us. They're on the other side. At unit 23C! We need to move."

Sam stood quickly, dropping the cards in his hands. Lea sat motionless.

"How many are out there? Do we have a chance fighting against them?" asked Sam.

"No way. There are too many. We either stay put and hope they can't open the unit—maybe they'll lose interest—or we leave. I say we leave. They'll stake out the place for sure, which will trap us inside. We can't stay here indefinitely."

"I'm with you. Let's grab the packs and move out. I'm just going to add more medical supplies and I'm ready."

"Be sure you put the water filtration unit back in your pack. It's on the table," said Jane.

"Got it."

Chapter Seven

Lea knew that insane asshole would find her. He always did. Somehow Tank managed to stick to her like glue, no matter how many times she tried to escape. His obsession with her had become a single focused drive.

She didn't understand why he'd kept her chained in the basement rather than killing her. It had dawned on her in the basement. She was smarter than Tank and he knew it. She never purposely bested him, it just happened naturally. Every time she figured something out before him or corrected him, another thread was sewn between them, binding them together. He needed to beat her. Until he had a victory over her, she would never be safe and neither would her parents.

She hurriedly shoved food, clothes and medical supplies in the pack her dad had given her. Something she'd just thought hit her like a ton of bricks. Tank would never leave any of them alone unless he got what he wanted.

"I'm not leaving," she announced.

"What do you mean you're not leaving?" asked Jane.

"I have to stay, or the two of you will never be safe."

"Not a chance. We won't leave you to that maniac," said Sam, grasping Lea's delicate hand.

"We need to stay together, for all of our safety, not just yours. Besides, there's no way we will let you go back to him after what we went through to get you," said Jane.

"You don't get it. Tank will never stop until he has me back. I'm all he wants. If I go with him, the two of you can escape to the HQ and come back for me."

"We're wasting precious time talking about this. You're not staying. End of discussion," said Jane.

Lea bristled at her mother's change in approach. Hearing the finality in her mother's voice made her even more determined to take her chances with Tank. Sam moved closer to Lea and rested his warm hand on her shoulder.

"Honey, I need you with me. I don't think I can handle knowing you're with Tank again. It would break my heart. I simply can't leave you here. If you stay, I stay. We can take our chances together."

Her dad's words always had a way of melting her heart. She knew he was serious. That he would stay with her and get killed in the process. He once again brought her back from that stubborn edge of anger elicited by her mom.

"Fine, Dad," she said before stuffing the last few items in her pack.

"Alright. It's settled. Let's get moving. Do you both have everything?" said Sam.

"Yeah," mother and daughter said in stony unison.

Chapter Eight

Sam lay flat on the cement floor of the storage unit, a mirror in one hand. He nodded to Jane to open the lift door. Slowly the door rolled quietly upward on its well-oiled tracks. When the door was high enough for him to effectively survey the surrounding area, Sam held his hand up, indicating she should stop. He quickly slipped a block underneath, wedging it open.

Mirror in hand, he surveyed the back of the facility. The distant shouts of men came from everywhere. It was difficult for Sam to determine the location of the men without stepping out of the unit. Leaving would be risky, but they didn't have a choice. The storage unit would become their tomb if they were discovered. All the New Order men had to do was light a fire in each of the adjacent storage units. The smoke alone would drive them out.

Seeing no one, Sam indicated it was time to move. Both Jane and Lea slid silently out of the unit as Sam held the door in place. He pushed their bug-out bags through next. Once outside the unit, Sam locked it and wedged the shims into place. He figured most people could pop off the lock, but if the door wouldn't budge, laziness would overcome desire to get into the unit. Or at least he hoped it would work. He hated the thought of giving up the storage locker and everything he'd stockpiled inside to Tank's crew. Once the police resolved the New Order problem and Tank was gone, the supplies would be critical to their survival.

The three of them slipped through a break in the chain-link fence, scurrying into the brush on the reverse side of the slope. The New Order men were everywhere. Sam made sure they escaped undetected before crawling back to bend the links on the fence to mask their escape route. Even with his multitool, he would have a hard time putting the links back together without his gloves on. The rough edges of the metal would cut his fingers to ribbons. He paused to dig out his gloves, instead finding his hand on the backup weapon he carried in his pack.

For a moment he considered an alternate plan. Nothing would give him more pleasure than shooting Tank, even if it meant giving up his life in the process. Ending Tank's reign of terror over their family was something he'd fantasied about long before the lights went out.

"What are you doing?" said Jane.

"Coming."

Sam made a few adjustments to the fence before joining Jane and Lea. Together, they moved silently down the embankment toward the creek and the trail that would take them away from Tank.

Chapter Nine

Tank leaned against the fence, watching his idiot crew crack open one locker after another. None of the lockers held anything useful. Just a bunch of discarded and forgotten junk, like farted-on sofas and dinged-up old tables. Unit 23C was mostly empty, much to Tank's dismay. A couple of wooden chairs and a broom were all they found in the Archers' unit—if it had in fact ever been the Archers' unit.

Just as Tank started to give up hope of finding anything, the answer occurred to him. If unit 23C was empty, they either no longer had a unit or they'd moved to a different one. Why would anyone move from one shit unit to another? All of the metal boxes seemed the same. Something didn't add up. Surveying the facility, he noticed something he hadn't caught before among the roughly two hundred storage units. Most were small, but a few of the rows held larger-sized bays. Unit 23C was a small one.

"Hey, let's move back here to the big ones. They must've upgraded to the deluxe shit-box models," yelled Tank on a hunch.

The men circled around the grounds to the back of the facility, which housed the larger units.

"Open the big ones only!" he shouted to the men as they moved to the rear of the grounds.

"Grab me the bolt cutters!" shouted Salem as he crouched down at the first unit.

Tank continued to walk the facility, sticking to the outer fence line, where he had the widest view of the place. The chain-link fence circled the entire storage lot in an unbroken line. Smoking a cigarette, Tank watched the men open locker after locker, finding more junk. Damn. Still nothing. Only one row of large lockers remained.

Taking the last draw of his cigarette, Tank flicked the butt into the air, creating a flash of hot orange ash in midair—his signature move. The glowing butt arched skyward before bouncing on the blacktop near the fence line. Glancing at the cigarette, his eyes were drawn to the fence. *Son of a bitch.*

The chain links had been cut from the ground to a point about three feet off the pavement, just large enough to peel back and squeeze through. Taking a closer look at the makeshift opening, Tank noticed that the grass and bushes outside the fence were trampled. *Someone very recently has been coming and going through the fence.*

"Hey, get over here. I found something!" shouted Tank to the men.

His men arrived a few seconds later.

"What is it?" shouted Salem.

"Look at this. Someone has been coming and going through here, probably stealing shit from the lockers. Let's follow their trail and see what we find."

"What trail?" said Salem as he pulled back the cut metal links.

"Just get moving, asshole," growled Tank.

Tank and the others slowly fought their way through the dense brush, every scrape and jab infuriating him. He would find Lea, and when he did, she would pay a steep price for making him go through all this.

"Do you think this connects to anything?" asked Bardo, a bearded heavyset man.

"How the fuck should I know? Do I look like Daniel fucking Boone?"

The man's face reddened at Tank's mockery. Good. Served that jackass right. He always asked too many stupid questions.

The woods seemed to close around them. Everywhere they turned looked the same to Tank. He couldn't be sure they weren't moving in circles.

"Let's head back up. They're gone."

As they scrambled up the embankment, Tank caught sight of a small red object. Leaning into the bushes, he picked up a cherry red hair scrunchy. Lea's scrunchy. That dumb bitch always wore her hair in the laziest way possible—a scrunchy. He had been right all along. They had been here. Moving through the fence onto the pavement, Tank redoubled his resolve to find Lea and teach her the most important lesson of her life.

Chapter Ten

Sergeant Dale Spencer urged the bike team on, toward Doris's house, leaving the foot mobile group behind to wait for their reconnaissance report. They streamed toward Doris's house with quiet precision. About a half mile from her home, Spencer halted the team. They needed to carefully scan the area before charging in. The New Order might have beaten them to the location.

"Alright, guys, listen up. We're approximately half a mile from the target. Green and Shorey, take a five-minute breather, then head out to conduct a stealthy reconnaissance of the immediate grounds surrounding the target. We need to know what we're getting into. If the New Order beat us to Doris's house, we'll have to take an entirely different approach."

"Got it," said Officer Green, between pulls of water.

"The rest of you start prepping your gear. Be ready to move out within thirty minutes."

"What about the bikes?" asked Officer Gould.

"Let's get the bikes off the trail. Turn them around so they're facing HQ, and lean them against the trees. Somewhere out of sight. If we need to make a hasty retreat, those should be ready to roll when we are."

Gould nodded. "I'll find a good spot."

Spencer pulled Officers Green and Shorey to the side.

"Move quickly, but carefully. Fall back immediately if you run into trouble. Remember. Your job is recon, not Rambo. Got it?"

"Yes, Sergeant," they said in unison.

"Alright, good luck."

Both Green and Shorey were young and fairly new to the force. He needed their athleticism and eyes, not their tactical acumen for this mission. Calculating the time to run from their current location to the house and back, adding the surveillance time, Spencer estimated the men should return in thirty to forty minutes. Setting his watch timer, Spencer hoped he didn't just send the two brave young men into an ambush.

A few moments later, the forest swallowed the two men, leaving Spencer to organize the rest of the group. They'd need to set up a perimeter while they waited. They were in hostile territory, a fact that he couldn't afford to forget. With a little luck, the group of officers on foot would catch up before Green and Shorey returned, giving him a sizable assault force.

~ ~ ~

Officer Seth Green grew weary as they approached Doris's house. He jogged closely behind Dan Shorey, but Shorey was a better, stronger runner than Green. The difference between the two men became painfully obvious the further they ran. The Evansville Police Department had become a second home to Green. He'd grown up near Evansville in a small town up north. Becoming a police officer and joining the force was the proudest day of his life. Finally he had something to believe in. Serving and protecting the people of Evansville was more than just a job to him, it was his life. The danger of their current situation did not bother Green, so long as his efforts served to protect the citizens.

"Hold up. We should lie low and crawl to a lookout position," said Shorey, taking a knee behind a tree.

Green caught a glimpse of the white farmhouse through the trees. The farm sat in the middle of a large expanse of open land, which he assumed was mostly ringed by the forest.

"Here's what we do. Seems like we're approaching the side of the house, which works out perfectly. You go to the right, viewing the front, and I'll make my way to the left, where I can scan the back. The only area we won't be able to thoroughly examine is the far side of the house."

"I think we'll be able to make a solid assessment watching the sectors visible from this side," said Green.

"I agree. Let's set our watches and plan to be here in fifteen," said Shorey.

"Got it."

"Remember. We don't engage any hostiles. No matter what we see."

"Roger that. See you in fifteen."

Green moved slowly through the forest, finally catching his breath. He opened his senses to the world around him in an effort to see and hear more as he approached. Anything could happen. He needed to be sharp. Judging by the cruelty inflicted on his brothers and sisters on the force by the New Order, he couldn't be too careful.

Settling into a good position along the edge of the forest, Green pulled out his binoculars. *Let's see what we have.* He moved his eyes methodically over each front window of the house. All of the windows were closed, which was a good sign. The first thing he'd do if he had to barricade a house like this would be to open the windows. Easier to hear and shoot someone that was approaching the house. Some of the windows were covered with curtains. Looked random to Green. Another good sign. He stared at each window for several seconds, looking for any movement. Nothing. Everything looked normal except the smashed blue flowerpot in the front yard.

The shed next to the house looked the same. The large roller doors on the shed were shut, and nothing moved behind the windows. The gigantic antenna attached to the shed explained why the chief wanted to keep this place out of New Order hands. If everything went well, the police could use that radio to communicate with other towns or the National Guard. They had precious little information about the world beyond the few surrounding towns. Figuring out what had happened to the electricity was on everyone's mind, but knowing how long the blackout would last was even more important.

After glancing at his watch, Green gave the house and grounds one more look. From what he could tell, the house, shed and approaching road were quiet. He swept the binoculars along the tree line on the other side of the clearing, finding an opening into the forest. It appeared to be a path of some sort, heading south toward Porter. The path must be the horse trail the others used to escape. He was about to head back to meet Shorey when he detected movement on the path.

He watched the path very carefully, looking for anything out of place. Sure enough, something stirred in the foliage. He watched and waited, focused intensely on the forest behind the trail. So intensely that he barely noticed Shorey creep up on him.

"Geez, Green. I've been looking all over for you. We were supposed to meet eight minutes ago."

"Get down. I think I have something."

Shorey quickly lay flat next to Green on the soft pine needles.

"Straight ahead at two o'clock. Something or someone is moving in this direction from the path."

"Got it."

"What do we do?"

"We wait and see, then report. Just like Spencer ordered us to do," said Shorey.

Green's hands sweated in anticipation, eyes trained on the dense brush of the path just beyond the trees.

Two people emerged from the horse trail. A twentysomething man and woman dressed in hiking gear.

"Hikers?"

"Looks like. Let's see what they do. Maybe they'll knock on the door. House was quiet on the back side."

"Same here until those two showed up."

Sure enough, the couple walked up the large wraparound porch and cautiously peered into the windows. The woman tried the front door without success. They walked around to the back of the house, out of sight.

"What do we do?" asked Green.

"Nothing. I say we give it another minute. See if anyone inside opens up. If not, seems like we just confirmed the house is empty."

The two sat silently watching. The couple moved back to the front of the house, grabbing peaches from one of the overburdened trees.

"Let's get back."

Chapter Eleven

Dale Spencer glanced at his watch for the fiftieth time since Green and Shorey had left. Sending the two of them out alone was a necessary risk, but it still made him extremely nervous. The team needed to be sure of the situation before they raced in.

The men approached from a different side than Spencer anticipated, throwing him off. They looked like they'd seen something.

"Glad to see you guys. What are we looking at?"

"The place is deserted. No sign of any New Order men in the vicinity," said Shorey.

"That's great. We should have a good shot at this, then."

"Except," said Green.

"Except?"

"Two hikers showed up just as we were leaving. We lingered to watch them. They peered into the windows and tried to get in the house. The place is buttoned up. And there was no reaction from inside to their arrival."

"That's good news. Did they leave, or are they still there?"

"They were sitting on the porch steps, eating peaches, when we left," offered Shorey. "They looked harmless enough."

"What're we looking at in terms of grounds and buildings?"

"Two structures, a house and a large work shed set out

approximately like this," said Green as he drew a map of Doris's property.

"What do the grounds look like? Is it clear or wooded?"

"The grounds are completely clear. Looks like some sort of working farm. As far as we can tell, the New Order would approach from here or here," said Green, pointing in turn to the horse trail and the road's entrance on the map.

"Nice work, guys. Grab your packs and gear up. We leave in ten."

Spencer walked over to the rest of the group. The remaining ten officers sat in small groups, chatting softly to break the tension. Controlling pre-operation jitters could make a huge difference in their success. The team needed to be sharp, not locked up with anticipation.

"We confirmed the house is still empty. Looks like we caught a break by beating the New Order here. This will give us time to get set up for their arrival. Be forewarned, Shorey and Green spotted two civilians. They may or may not be there when we show up. Either way, we need to ensure they don't get caught in any crossfire."

The group listened intently while prepping the last of their tactical gear.

"The rules of engagement are as follows: we shoot the New Order on sight if they approach the house. We don't have the capacity to take prisoners at this point. The chief ordered there to be no prisoners. Are we clear?"

"What do we do if one of them is wounded?" said Green.

"I'm not executing anybody," said another officer.

"Nobody's asking you to execute anyone," said Spencer. "But I need to know you're willing to open fire first, without issuing any warning to the New Order. The house is important, and we'll need every bit of advantage we can muster. Does anyone have a problem with that?"

A few of them muttered, but nobody refused. Spencer knew his officers would be uncomfortable killing the New Order men on sight; however, they had no practical way to secure and feed prisoners. Trying to re-create a prison system in their current predicament would likely result in more police casualties. The decision was made and they would execute it.

"You didn't really answer the question," said an officer.

Spencer considered his response, not wanting to lose any of his officers.

"Here's how I see it. We're at war with the New Order. If an enemy combatant falls wounded on the battlefield, it's not our responsibility to patch them up. We'll take away their weapons so they're no longer a threat and then assess their situation. My number one priority is removing the threat. I won't execute anyone, either, but I won't risk your lives to save any of those scumbags. Frankly, we'll be lucky if we can take care of our own wounded, let alone theirs. That's the situation. If you're not okay with this, I need to know right now. No judgment."

He locked eyes with each of his officers for a few seconds, gauging their reactions. From what he could tell, he hadn't lost anyone.

"We move out in five."

~ ~ ~

Deputy Kara Lovell walked behind Seth Green as the group approached the house. A veteran police officer in the tactical unit, Lovell had seen her share of hostile takedowns. She double-checked her vest pockets for her supplies. Extra ammunition, weapons, a hunting knife and two flash grenades were neatly packed away. Double-checking her load out usually calmed her pre-mission nerves. Not this time.

She had never been on a mission that involved shooting first and leaving survivors to die. This did not sit well with her, but she couldn't see a way around it. The situation required a dramatically different approach than what they were all accustomed to, but leaving the wounded to die felt unethical. She hoped it didn't come to that.

The team approached the tree line near the edge of the clearing. Sergeant Spencer sent two men to the front of the house and two to the back. The others waited and watched. The two in the front quickly pushed their way through the door and into the house. The back door must have been breached as well, although she could not tell from her vantage point. Shouts of, "Clear!" rang through the house, echoing in the forest.

One of the breaching team members stood on the front porch and gave them a thumbs-up.

"Let's move in," said Sergeant Spencer.

The group gathered on the front yard under the shade of a tree. Their sergeant and team leader scoped the surrounding area. The four members of the breaching team joined their huddle.

"Here's what we have. Two points of approach, the horse trail over there and the road right here," said Spencer while pointing to the openings in the forest. "We need to cover both points while also planning for any surprises the New Order throws in our direction. Green and Shorey, I want you on the forward observation post. Hike about a half mile up the horse trail and wait. The first sign of the New Order, you radio it in. Markus, Lovell and Peterson, I want you in the second-story windows, there and there. Roy and Stacy take the shed. The rest of you filter in behind the house and well."

The team quickly disbursed to their assigned locations and waited. For Lovell, waiting was always the hardest part of a tactical operation. Ensconced in a forward-facing second-story bedroom, Lovell made preparations for the attack. She created a makeshift bunker with the mattress and laid out her extra weapons in a way that would facilitate her quick access.

~ ~ ~

Dale Spencer circled through the various points where he'd placed his officers. They were all well trained and highly effective. He had every confidence they would be able to hold the house. His radio cracked to life.

"Sergeant, it's Miller. You copy?"

Deputy Miller headed the foot mobile team they'd left behind on the trail.

"This is Spencer, copy."

"We're about a mile away. Over."

"The pizza is in the oven," said Spencer, using their prearranged code for all clear.

"Sounds good."

The men and women would arrive within fifteen minutes. Their numbers would really bolster the team. He would spread them around the forest, house, outside the shed and house, and even under the porch. Reflecting on the tactical advantage the police had over the untrained New Order thugs gave Spencer some hope that the team might walk out of this fight mostly intact.

Chapter Twelve

Travis Marks drove the first of four New Order cars. The Boss had become convinced that the cops were moving their survivors out of town. Nothing pissed off the Boss more than thinking someone was getting the better of him. As far as Travis was concerned, he couldn't give a shit, so long as the cops were gone and they could continue to live like kings.

Trying to drive parallel to the trail had been a little bit of a challenge for him and the other three drivers—since no road actually followed the damn trail! They'd zigzagged back and forth on roads close to the trail, following its general direction. Periodically, the men on the trail would emerge from the forest to indicate they were still going in the right direction. Not exactly a stellar plan.

They were moving at a snail's pace. After a few hours of this nonsense, Travis had finally thought to look in the glove box of the grandma car he was driving for a map. Sure enough, he found a well-worn local map stuffed between a bunch of receipts and car-related paperwork. The map told him everything he needed to know. They'd travel in a northerly direction, looking for roads that led to properties along the trail. The only problem was that they didn't see many homes or driveway entrances outside town. They'd have to look at the map and guess where a road or driveway might take them, hoping it would be connected to the trail. So much for expediency.

Eventually most of the guys hiking the trail got too tired from heat and exertion to keep walking. They squeezed their sorry asses into the cars like a bunch of clowns in a circus. Only he wasn't laughing. The vehicle now reeked like a toxic combination of body odor and bad breath. Annoyance mounted as the miles slowly ambled by, one more boring than the next. He had half a mind to force the extra men back out onto the trail, but he refrained. Most of the men in the car were stupid, angry, and armed, a dangerous combination even on a good day.

Thoughts of slamming the car into a utility pole filled Travis's head as the men got more obnoxious and mouthy. He couldn't blame them. They were driving roughly parallel to the trail, he hoped, but the road had given them nothing. Fuck it. Maybe it was time to call it good. Best he could do with a car full of smelly losers. Finally, a lone mailbox sat on the side of the road, indicating a residence. If he had been looking at the boring scenery or lighting a cigarette, he might have missed it.

"Reece! Check it out," said Travis to Reece, the front-seat passenger.

"You think we should stop?"

"It's the only house we've seen on this long fucking boring drive. So, yeah, we stop."

Travis slowed the vehicle and turned into the driveway. The other three cars followed closely behind.

"Why're we stopping?" said Twinky from the backseat.

"Why the fuck do you think we're stopping? The Boss wanted us to check out every house along that trail," said Travis, finally hitting his stupid quotient for the day.

The long drive snaked through the dense forest, leaving Travis unsure where they were heading. It seemed like a lot of driveway for just one house. Then the large white farmhouse came into view.

"Well, well, what do we have here! Look at this place!" said Travis.

"Yeah, makes where we're staying look like a shit box," said Reece.

"Doesn't look like anyone is home either. Maybe the Boss was wrong."

"Only one way to find out!" said Twinky, eliciting a round of barely contained excitement from the backseat.

Travis pulled the car through the circular drive like a millionaire pulling up to his mansion. He had always wanted to do that. Growing up in the projects, no one had a circular drive, or any driveway for that matter. To Travis, the driveway alone was a luxury. The other cars crept into place behind him, the armed men piling noisily out of the vehicles.

~ ~ ~

Dale Spencer stood in the front bedroom, behind Officer Lovell, and watched as four vehicles turned into the driveway. The heavily armed men that climbed out of the cars resembled typical gang members. They pounded the tops and hoods of the vehicles, hooting and hollering like a pack of hungry jackals.

"What should we do, Sergeant?" whispered Lovell.

"Give them a minute to get away from the cover of their vehicles."

"New Order" was spray painted on two of the cars, leaving no doubt in Spencer's mind who they were.

He lifted his handheld radio and whispered to Officer Stacy, who was in the shed with Officer Roy. "Hold your fire until I give the order."

"Copy that, sir," replied Stacy.

The New Order goons gathered in a loose group near the tree in the front yard. He wanted them a little closer to the house to give the few officers only armed with pistols a better chance to effectively join the first volley, but he couldn't risk the possibility that the group might disburse. If they didn't take the men down now, while they stood around in a tight group, the advantage would be lost.

"Fire! All hands open fire!"

In unison, the police hidden in the house, tree lines and shed poured bullets into the New Order men. Some of the bullets were personal, retribution for personal losses. Most were in service to the innocent civilians who would be saved by ending the New Order's savage reign.

The first wave of shots caught the gang unaware. Several men dropped at once, landing on the ground where they had once stood. The survivors quickly ran behind the vehicles and returned fire. Bullet after bullet hit the house, shattering windows and punching through the outer walls. Splinters of wood and glass showered Spencer as he methodically pressed the trigger of his rifle, moving from target to target. With the New Order gang pinned down, it was time to maneuver into position to end this.

"Spicer and Marz, get behind them. I want fire superiority from all sides!" barked Spencer into the radio.

Over his rifle sights, he could see his officers rushing through the underbrush to close off New Order's only avenue of escape. Before they could get into position and effectively take out the remaining five men crouched behind the cars, one of the men climbed into the front vehicle and tore off down the driveway. Bullets hit the gravel road, chasing the car with no success.

"Watch your fire!" barked Spencer over the radio. "Marz and Spicer are out there!"

The two officers fired several shots at the fleeing vehicle, shattering the rear window, but failing to stop the escape. Having heard the gunfire from their rear, the gang members panicked and repositioned themselves among the cars, effectively exposing themselves to gunfire from every direction. Within seconds it was over, the last New Order gunman taking several hits to the torso before bouncing between bumpers and coming to a rest on the driveway. The yard became quiet once again.

Spencer swept the forest line and surrounding areas with his binoculars. Nothing moved. No additional men were coming.

"All teams report your status!"

"Overlook one. All clear." The south forest and side of the house were clear.

"Robby two—clear." The north forest and rear of the house were clear.

"Central three clear." The shed and front of the house were clear.

"All units stand down," said Spencer with relief.

Spencer and Lovell walked out of the bedroom to join the others in the front yard. The second front bedroom sat in quiet contrast to the rest of the house, which was crawling with excitement.

"Peterson? You okay?" yelled Lovell down the hallway toward the officer stationed in that bedroom's window.

No response.

Spencer glanced at Lovell and said, "I'll check. I know you two were close."

"I need to do this for him."

Bret Peterson's lifeless body lay supine in an expanding pool of blood—a reddish-black hole in the middle of his forehead.

"I'm so sorry, Kara. He was a good man and a great officer."

The room seemed to have a stillness of its own as Lovell held her friend and cried. Glancing at the cops gathering on the front lawn, Spencer decided to give her some privacy.

Chapter Thirteen

By Spencer's count, nineteen New Order men lay scattered around the yard. It was a dent in the New Order's ranks, but not a huge one.

"Alright, people, let's get the bodies in a pile about thirty feet into the eastern tree line. We'll bury them later. I don't want to draw any scavengers to the house. We'll be jumpy enough at night," said Spencer to the group of officers gathering in front of the house. "Line the cars on this side of the driveway, facing west. Take all usable weapons and ammunition off the bodies and out of the cars."

Standing off to the side, he decided to check in with Green and Shorey. They were sent south, down the horse trail, as the team's eyes and ears. If anything came down the trail, they would have alerted the team.

"Green, it's Sergeant. You copy?"

Nothing.

"Green? Come in, it's Sergeant."

Nothing but static.

"What's up, Sergeant?" asked Lovell, appearing on the porch.

"I'm not sure, probably nothing. I can't seem to get Green to come in. He didn't respond during the last report."

"They hiked pretty far into the woods. Maybe they're out of range?"

"Yeah, maybe."

He thought about sending a group into the woods to check on

them, but if they had somehow fallen prey to a silent ambush, he'd just as likely lose anyone else that ventured into the woods.

Turning to Officer Roy, Spencer yelled, "Roy, get the radio in the shed up and running. We lost communications with Shorey and Green."

~ ~ ~

Officers Green and Shorey walked side by side along the horse trail. They heard the gunfire, followed by the "all clear" reports. Shorey also reported that all appeared clear on the trail, but he'd never heard back from Sergeant Spencer.

"I think we should head back," whispered Green. "If they can't hear our transmissions, we're no good as scouts."

He was right. They couldn't see very far in front of them on the trail. If a group appeared, they'd have no choice but to stand and fight, hoping their gunshots would warn the police at the house. Turning to run, they risked getting shot in the back before they were in radio range. Both options relied on gunshots to warn the other officers. Both options would likely get them both killed. Spencer wouldn't send more officers blindly into the forest. They needed to get back into radio range. Walking down this trail, even as quietly and carefully as they'd been, didn't seem like such a good idea anymore.

"I agree," said Shorey. "What do you think happened back at the house?"

"I don't know. My guess is that it went our way. The whole thing didn't last very long. I'm just hoping—"

Green dropped to his knees on the forest floor, a bloody arrow protruding from the front of his neck. His stunned eyes pleaded with Shorey as he gurgled through gushing blood for air.

"Holy shit!" screamed Shorey, crouching as low as he could without lying down.

He needed to find cover fast. *But from which direction?* The arrow seemed to come from their rear, but he couldn't be sure. He started to sweep the immediate area around him for the threat.

"Drop it, asshole! And don't none of you shits shoot him! He's mine!" yelled a sneering voice from behind.

"What are you doing? Just cap the pig!"

"Nope. We're bringing him back to the Boss. He'll love to get his hands on fresh cop meat. And looks like we've got a live one here," said Burner, to a round of laughter.

"How much further should we go, man? I'm getting tired of walking. This sucks!" said one of the men.

The other six men nodded and grumbled their assent.

"We go until we meet up with the guys. From the gunfire we just heard, sounds like they leveled the pigs sitting in their little hidey-hole. I intend to ride back to the Boss in style, with this asshole as my prize," said Burner.

Strong hands yanked Shorey to his knees. The hands spun him around, and he was pistol-whipped a few times before someone pulled him to his feet. His face had been hit so hard that his eyes started to immediately swell. Green's radio crackled to life. *Crap, not now.*

"Green, it's Sergeant. You copy?"

"Green? Come in, it's Sergeant."

Shorey stole a glance at the man they called Burner. He seemed to be deep in thought.

~ ~ ~

Lovell heaved another bucket of cool water from the well, placing it on the wet grass. She had never tasted anything so good. They had been rationing the limited supply of water at the HQ. Creating fresh water at HQ involved hauling and boiling water from the nearby lake. A chore that became more arduous by the day. Everyone tried to drink only what they needed to avoid creating more work. Guzzling cup after cup of fresh well water felt like a guilty pleasure.

Sitting on the edge of a rock, she looked across the landscape. Doris had a great setup. The farm boasted a beautiful house, large garden, water well and plenty of fruit trees. She could get used to this.

She let her mind relax for a moment, taking in the quiet, idyllic scene, until one of the Porter cops dropped to the grass. Her mind didn't register a problem until another officer fell, and the sound of rapid-fire gunshots washed across the clearing. *Holy shit!* The men and women in their company ran for cover, darting in zigzag patterns to try to make themselves a difficult target. She watched as her fellow officers were gunned down.

She scrambled to locate the source of the shooting. Flashes appeared in the southern tree line near the horse trail. She had no radio and no way to communicate to the other officers. Lining up the first target, she fired, hitting the mark. One of the New Order men looked down at his dead friend and turned in her direction to return fire. She nailed him in the chest, center mass, knocking him into the thick foliage.

Unable to acquire a new target, she fired bullet after bullet into the group of men hiding in the trees, hoping to at least give the other officers cover. Her suppressing fire worked. The police started shooting back as a group, bullet after bullet ripping through the trees. The gunfire stopped just as suddenly. She knew they needed to be cautious about the amount of ammunition they used. Maybe they were trying to assess the situation.

Two figures emerged from the shadows, the one in front waving a white cloth. She immediately recognized Officer Shorey. The man hidden behind him held Shorey by the shoulder, a gun likely stuck in his back.

"Stop shooting or this asshole goes down too!" yelled the man.

She remained still, centering her rifle sights on the men. No shot. From her angle, she had just as much chance of hitting Shorey.

"Let him go and we'll talk!" yelled one of the officers.

"No way, hoss. He stays with me. We're going to take a little drive together."

The man made his way across the lawn toward the cars, dragging his human shield with him.

~ ~ ~

Mark Jordan and Joe Price were on the horse trail, headed to Doris's house, when the gunfire erupted. Knowing the other police were in danger, the two ran the remaining mile to the edge of the clearing, pausing, exhausted, to assess the situation. From what he could tell, the police had won their first battle. The New Order bodies had been gathered in a pile next to the porch, and a police officer maneuvered the last vehicle into a convoy pointed west, down the driveway.

Joe raised his hand and started to announce their arrival when Mark grabbed him and pulled him down. Joe hadn't seen the first man drop, but Mark did. A furious gunfight erupted, lasting a few seconds before abruptly ending. *Bizarre.* He crawled to the edge of the tree line and observed, his rifle barely protruding from the brush. After a brief moment, two men walked out of the forest, waving a white cloth. Mark centered his rifle's scope on the men.

"Shit," he muttered.

"What?" said Joe, who had crawled next to him.

"Hostage situation."

"Can you take the shot?"

"I don't know."

Mark had the New Order man in his sights, but the officer's head kept appearing in the crosshairs when he started to apply pressure to the trigger. Mark needed to wait until he had a perfect, predictably unhindered shot, if that ever happened. The New Order man did a decent job of shielding himself with his hostage. Mark had one advantage in this situation. The guy didn't know he was in the crosshairs of a former sniper. Given enough time, he'd make a mistake. The problem was time. The two of them were headed toward the vehicles, where time ended for the hostage. If he didn't find a shot in the next several seconds, the officer was as good as dead.

He kept the crosshairs on the New Order man, breathing as shallowly as possible with most of the pressure off his rifle's two-stage trigger. *Just give me something.* Finally, as the gang member stuffed the hostage into the car, Mark's opportunity arrived. With deadly precision, Mark took the best shot he had. The sound of his rifle cracked through the air as the man slumped to the ground next to a blood-splattered, open car door.

Chapter Fourteen

Jane hiked fast along the horse trail, heading north toward the HQ. They needed to put the maximum amount of distance between themselves and the New Order. She could hardly believe that Tank had found them. It was like a living nightmare. He must have gone through their things and found some evidence of the locker, unless Lea told him.

"Are you sure you didn't say anything to Tank about the locker?" she asked Lea.

"Geez, Mom. How many times do I have to say that I didn't! I hardly knew what you guys were doing there, let alone the location and locker number. Really, it wasn't me."

"Maybe he found something at the house. A receipt or something?" offered Sam.

"I don't know. You were really careful not to keep any records of the locker. I remember you always shredded the statements after you paid the bill."

"I did. But I'm not perfect. Something could have slipped through the cracks. It really doesn't matter at this point. We needed to move and are moving. End of story," said Sam with finality.

Jane knew she was obsessing over how Tank had found them and that it didn't matter at this point. Still, she was convinced that Lea must have told Tank and wouldn't admit it. For now, she would take

Sam's cue and leave it alone. Nothing good would come of her pursuing it. She glanced over her shoulder at Sam and smiled. He returned the smile with a faint nod.

"Can we take a break? I need to go to the bathroom," asked Lea, exasperated. "I could use a break, too."

"It's been several hours since we left the locker. At this rate, I think they'd need to be driving to keep up with us. What do you say, Jane? We take fifteen?" asked Sam playfully.

"You're right, we've made good time. Let's take fifteen minutes."

Lea had dropped her overloaded pack before Jane stopped talking. She trotted off the path into the woods.

"I'll be right back!"

"Don't go far!" yelled Jane as Lea disappeared into the forest.

The few minutes Lea was gone was the only time she and Sam had been alone since rescuing their daughter. She moved close to Sam, circling her arms around him.

"Thanks for getting me out of the *how did Tank find us* rut," she said.

Smiling, Sam kissed her head gently and said, "You really didn't seem to be getting anywhere with that besides upsetting Lea. For what it's worth, I don't think she told Tank anything. Otherwise, he would've broken into the locker long before we got there."

"I thought of that too, but it just seems far-fetched that he found us. I overheard one of his men shouting that they found locker number 23C. He clearly knew where we had been."

"I'm hoping they get frustrated and leave. I'd hate to lose all of our supplies. We might need them once things go back to normal. Or whatever they go to after the New Order is gone. I'm not sure how well equipped the HQ is or how many people will be sharing the limited resources they may have."

Lea reappeared from her bathroom break. Sam and Jane's time was over.

"Dad, how much further do you think we have to walk?" said Lea.

"As long as we remain on the correct trail, I think we should get there within the next few hours."

"Good. I'm getting sick of carrying this pack."

Jane reluctantly pulled away from Sam's arms before stretching her body. Hiking with a full pack had seemed so charming two weeks ago when they'd first left for their backpacking trip. Little did she know. Now the darn thing seemed like a cruel punishment. The contents of the pack made her extremely fortunate, given the circumstances, so she tried to focus more on their good fortune and less on her heat blisters. Heaving the pack onto her slight frame, she turned to Sam and Lea.

"You guys ready?"

Jane waited for Sam and Lea to pass her and take the lead. Father and daughter walked ahead, chatting amicably. Smiling to herself, she knew she was lucky—not just for the contents of the pack, but for having her family intact. Many people had lost more than just their canned goods to the New Order. She felt exceedingly fortunate.

Chapter Fifteen

Sergeant Dale Spencer surveyed the carnage left by the New Order counterattack. Two of his officers had been killed in the driveway and an additional five were wounded. Doris's living room had been turned into a makeshift emergency room. They carried a field medical kit, which came in handy to patch up the less severe wounds, but two of his men needed the kind of care they couldn't provide at the house. From what he could tell, they required surgery.

Immediately after the shooting stopped, he formed a rotation to staff the perimeter guard. His officers ringed the house and nearby forest at strategic intervals. Each carried a handheld radio to signal a warning. They would not be caught off guard again if he could help it. The remaining men and women buried the dead, tended to the wounded and assessed their supply situation. The most important task fell to Officers Donnelly and Pritty. They were getting Doris's radio up and working.

Walking into what was now called the "comms shed," Spencer had to take some time for his eyes to adjust to the gloom.

"How's it going in here? Is the radio working again?" asked Spencer.

"It seems like we have everything working. We're able to test it by squawking one of the handhelds. The signal was sent and received loud and clear on both ends," said Officer Jason Donnelly.

"That's great news. If you're sure it'll work, we should turn it off and wait for tonight to communicate with the chief. I'm sure he's anxious for a status update," said Spencer.

"There isn't more we can do without risking a statewide communication. The antenna is crazy strong on this thing," said Officer Howard Pritty.

"Nice work, guys. There's talk about lunch. Whenever you're ready, we're meeting in the backyard."

Spencer gave them a stoic smile. If any of them had any reservations about how the day had gone down, nobody said a word about it. Securing this location, with its radio and close proximity to Porter, was tactically critical. The rapid arrival of the New Order thugs only underscored its importance. They would need everything the farm had to offer in order to fight back and regain their towns. Everyone involved in the mission knew that. They couldn't afford to lose this place.

Chapter Sixteen

Johnny sat in stunned silence as Travis recounted what had happened at the farmhouse. When Johnny realized the cops had mounted a coordinated effort to fight back against the New Order, he could barely contain his excitement. For his own safety, he needed to at least appear neutral in the eyes of the Boss. If the Boss knew he celebrated the death of the New Order men and the possibility that the cops were on the offensive, he would be killed on the spot.

Listening to Travis, Johnny tried to figure out how many police officers were involved in the attack.

"You should've seen it, man. They just started fucking shooting. Whatever happened to our rights? Shit. They didn't care if they killed us all. Might've too, if I hadn't jumped in the car at the last second," said Travis.

"Fuck them! They think they're going to kill my soldiers! Well, let them try to come into Porter! I'll skin them alive with my own hands if that's what it takes!" shouted the Boss.

Several loyal New Order men nodded and mumbled their agreement with the Boss's lunacy. Glancing at Brown, Johnny saw a flicker of what appeared to be hope. Or was that ambition? Hard to tell with Brown.

"No way will they be able to take over the town. We've got this shit locked down!" said Brown.

"Yeah!" shouted another man excitedly.

65

"Those fucking cops are no match for us. Never were. We're gonna fight the pigs right where they are, tonight. Spoc, get the guys ready! We're gonna show those assholes who they're dealing with. No way can we let this one lie! We hit them hard tonight!" shouted the Boss.

His actions and words had become increasingly erratic over the past days. Less proactive and more reactive. The guy didn't respond well when things weren't one hundred percent under his control. Johnny predicted that he'd unravel fast if the police directly attacked the town. He couldn't wait.

"Fuck yeah! I know exactly where they are. We can hit them at night, all creepy and secretive. They won't know what hit them!" shouted Travis, to another round of jeers from the hardened men.

Johnny slowly made his way toward the back of the group and faded off into another part of the Porter police station. He knew from experience that when the guys started getting excited, it was time to clear out. Once the New Order men started drinking, anything could happen. He never saw a wilder, meaner bunch than these men. Getting away now would ensure he wasn't part of their drunken activities. Plus, he could use the chaotic moment to get the bag of supplies Brown had stashed for him in the radio room.

"Where're you going?"

Johnny froze, turning slowly around to face Brown. "I need to get the supplies to my grandma. Can you cover for me?"

"Why should I?"

"What do you mean? I need your help?"

"I don't want to get my ass capped for you and your grandma!" said Brown.

"I'll be back within the hour. Just watch out for me."

"All right, man. Just hurry," said Brown, annoyed.

Johnny slipped out of the station's back door and ran as fast as he could across town to deliver the supplies to his grandmother, Rusty. The couple of cans and bars should keep her going for a few more days. Seeing her lose so much weight really worried Johnny. He wished he could do more for her but knew that was impossible.

~ ~ ~

Brown leaned back in the cracked leather chair he'd dragged into the communications room. The radio sat silent now. The New Order had been running so many lights without any thought about the fuel supply. Now they needed to be more cautious about their use of the supplies—especially the generator. Brown knew the men were too stupid to understand the concept of rationing.

It was only a matter of time before their thinning food stockpile vanished. The men gorged like they had arrived at a buffet thirty minutes before closing time. They had no concern for tomorrow, which was probably why they were in prison in the first place. Same thing had landed his own ass in jail. He wasn't going to make that mistake again. Big picture or little picture.

Brown had slowly saved a few cans here, a bottle of water there—whatever he could get his hands on—stashing it safely in the house he'd taken over. No one seemed to notice. He ate with the guys and enjoyed the bounty while secretly preparing for a time when the food went dry. He'd slip away at that point, the place guaranteed to descend into sheer madness. Not that it wasn't already an insane asylum.

After hearing Travis's version of the day's events, Brown knew he'd made the right decision to stay back from the raid on Doris's house. He had a gut feeling it would not go well, but he didn't realize the cops would wipe them out down to the last man. Now more than ever he needed to let the police know he was on their side and not the New Order's. That was big-picture thinking. It was only a matter of time before they came back into town, and when they did, he did not intend to be on the receiving end of a bullet.

Chapter Seventeen

Sam swatted mosquitoes as he searched for the camp's entrance. They had left the storage unit in such a hurry that he hadn't thought to restock their bug spray. Their packs contained the mostly used bottles from the backpacking trip. Slapping his arms again made him even angrier at their current situation. He had prepared for everything, even having the foresight to put the bulk of their supplies in a second location. He just hadn't counted on having to leave the location so quickly. If he'd just had another day, they could have taken so much more.

"Hold up, ladies. I think this is the entrance," said Sam, pointing to a smallish dirt road.

Following the map had forced them off the horse trail and onto a paved road for the last mile. He'd felt entirely exposed on the road, so they'd taken to the forest, a decision that quickly became one of his least popular so far. They just couldn't risk being spotted on the road. They'd gone through too much and come too far to screw up something that simple. Sam slapped the side of his neck. Even he was starting to lose it. If the map was correct, the camp's entrance should be just down the road.

"We're almost there," he said.

"You said that ten minutes ago," said Lea.

Sam mumbled a few choice words under his breath. They came upon a dirt road in the trees, which looked well used.

"This might be it," he said, walking up the dirt road to the pavement.

He couldn't find a camp sign or any indication where one had stood.

"It's not marked. I don't know. Maybe we should keep walking. I would think a camp would have a sign of some sort," said Jane.

"Me too, but this has to be it. Look at the map." Sam brought the map to Jane.

They huddled together, their hips touching. A wave of desire washed over Sam as he stood close to his wife.

"You see? We came out of the forest's trail here, and now, we should be around this point. The camp is on the map and so is the road. I say we try it," said Sam.

"Me too. I can't bear walking another inch. Especially if we're going in the wrong direction, again," said Lea.

"Okay, but let's be cautious. We have no idea what we're walking into."

"Do you think we should draw our weapons?" asked Sam.

"No, let's just unholster them. Weapons drawn might get us shot. We just need to be ready in case the situation spirals in the wrong direction. Lea, you get behind us."

The three walked cautiously down the dirt road. In the distance a chain-link gate blocked the road, preventing anyone from wandering in or driving through.

"Now what?" asked Sam.

"Looks like there's a call box. We should just ring for someone."

Sam and Jane turned toward their daughter at the exact moment. *Did she really just forget there is no power?*

"Oops. My bad. It's so habitual to keep expecting the power to be on and for things to work," said Lea, laughing.

"Stop right there! Drop your weapons!" shouted a lone female voice.

The three of them hesitated, not wanting to give up their only means of defense. They could have stumbled onto anyone's hideout. Sam's stomach churned at the thought of the three of them being turned away, stripped of their packs and weapons. He glanced at Jane. He could tell she was thinking the same thing. *Should we run?* A few tense seconds passed.

"You heard me! Drop your weapons. Slowly!" the woman yelled forcefully.

Without moving to throw down her weapon, Jane shouted, "We're looking for Camp Hemlock. I'm Jane Archer."

Sam knew what Jane just did. She'd identified herself and the camp, thereby alerting the listener that she was a fellow officer. If this was the right place, Sam knew they would get in. If not, Jane managed to not give away any information.

"Jane? Holy shit!"

A lone woman trotted out from behind the gate, moving to unlock it.

"Joyce!"

Jane ran to her friend. The women quickly embraced.

"I had no idea you were heading up here. Charlie told us about your daughter. We all hoped you would be okay. Is this her?"

"Yes, our daughter, Lea, and my husband, Sam."

"Nice to meet you both. Let's get you inside so I can secure the gate."

The gate rolled shut with a rickety metallic clang. The gate looked like the sort of thing to keep out bored teenagers, not murderous convicts. Sam hoped the HQ would be a place they could rest easy; so far he'd seen very little indication that they were truly safe.

~ ~ ~

Jane followed her friend closely as they walked the dirt road to the interior of the camp. Distant voices echoed off the trees. The glimmer of Lake Sparrow sat in the distance.

"We weren't sure we had the right place. There's no sign," said Jane.

"Chief had us take it down, along with the road signs. Better to hide the location," said Joyce.

"How long have you been here?"

"Soon after things started spiraling out of control, Chief had us strip the station and move here on foot."

"Are Bret and Suzi with you?" asked Jane, referring to Joyce's husband and daughter.

"Only Suzi. Bret was one of the first men dragged into the streets. After it happened, Suzi and I hid, finally finding our way to the station just as everything was being dismantled."

Joyce's face was tight with worry and grief. She had been through so much more than Jane. Placing her hand on Joyce's shoulder, Jane said, "I'm so sorry, Joyce. That must have been awful. I can't even imagine."

"It's been hard, but at least we're here, relatively safe," said Joyce, trying to hold back tears.

"Relatively? What do you mean?" asked Sam.

"The New Order moved up the horse trail in this direction. Apparently they were headed to Doris Venture's house, the first safe house coming out of Porter."

"We know it very well. We stayed with her on our way home," said Sam.

"Right, with everything going on, I forgot you were away."

"Is she okay? Doris, I mean? Has she been moved up here?" asked Jane.

"We're not sure yet. A team went down this morning to get her out of there. Hey, Chief!" said Joyce, waving to their chief. "He can fill you in on the details. I'm on the watch rotation and need to get back to my post. I'm glad you guys made it here."

Chief Carlisle moved quickly in their direction. Jane felt her shoulders relax, just a little. The chief was the best leader she'd ever served under. He ran the police with a calm, steady hand. He was also one of the best tactical planners she ever met. She knew that if anyone could help their towns regain civility, it was their chief.

"Jane! Nice to see you!" he said, shaking her hand.

"You remember my husband, Sam, and daughter, Lea."

"Of course. I'm so happy the three of you are safe and sound. I heard about your trek out of the mountains."

"We're pretty relieved to be here too," said Sam.

"Joyce said a team went to Doris's house to get her. What's going on?" asked Jane.

"Come on. Let's head inside and we can chat. I don't want some of the younger kids to overhear us."

The four walked to an immaculate, spacious post-and-beam camp lodge. The place looked more like a woodsy four-star hotel than a kids' camp. The back side of the building had large floor-to-ceiling windows overlooking the vast expanse of Lake Sparrow. Gleaming hardwood floors stretched across the entire building. A grand two-story fieldstone fireplace framed the room.

"This is a kids' camp? I should've listened to the two of you when you wanted to send me away for a few weeks in the summer. Looks like I really missed out!" said Lea.

"Don't worry. You didn't miss anything. We would've sent you to the rustic camp down the street." Sam smiled.

They moved outside to the large wraparound deck and sat on a picnic table overlooking the lake.

"As you know, we moved here to get away from the New Order. The New Order took us completely by surprise. We were adjusting to the loss of power, rendering aid as needed, when they just rolled into town and started cutting us down. I had to make a quick decision. Stay and fight, with the odds stacked against us, or withdraw and regroup for an organized counterattack. I went with the second option, because I felt it best served the people of Evansville in the long run. If the New Order had wiped us out at the outset, nothing could protect the people. At least now we have a fighting chance. And a good one at that.

"The first wave of our resistance started today by securing Doris Venture's house. One of the Porter police officers named Gayle Jones is assembling veterans outside Porter to push into the town from the south. The plan is to hit the New Order in Porter from both the north and south in a coordinated attack. Probably within a day or two."

Jane sat looking at the chief in stunned silence. She knew the police would eventually mount a resistance, she just didn't know when. It all seemed to be moving so fast.

"How did you know about the New Order's plan to hit Doris's house?" asked Jane.

"We dismantled and brought a portion of our radio from the station. We had to connect to the camp's antenna, however. There was a small radio here. It must've been here for emergencies. We really couldn't hear anything outside of the camp until Doris's radio started broadcasting."

"I helped get that radio operational with Charlie," said Sam. "It has one hell of an antenna. You might be able to contact county for help."

"One step at a time," said the chief.

"Is Charlie here?" asked Jane.

"Haven't seen him yet."

She had a sinking feeling hearing that. He should have been here by now.

"What's happening at Doris's house? Has the New Order arrived?" asked Sam.

"Not sure yet. We're maintaining radio silence until tonight. Doris's radio is so powerful, we can't chance being overheard by the New Order. So far, we believe the HQ's location is unknown to them. We'll know more about the situation at Doris's house tonight, just after midnight. Until then, let's get you settled."

Chapter Eighteen

Charlie unconsciously picked up the pace as he neared HQ. He was in excellent physical condition from the daily runs, swims and bike rides he enjoyed. Getting to HQ and being reunited with Gayle was the only thing on his mind as the hours passed on their hike from Scott's house to HQ.

"Charlie! Hey, man, can we ease up on the pace?" asked an obviously winded Mike.

"I don't think I've moved this fast since the two-for-one sale on shoes at Marshalls," said Barbara with a smile.

"Sorry about that. I guess we've been moving pretty fast. We're very close to the HQ. Let's stop for a minute so I can alert them we're coming," said Charlie.

Charlie pulled the handheld radio out of his pack. Using the predetermined channel and squawking sequence, he attempted to reach HQ.

"What are you doing? Doesn't the radio work?" asked Doris.

"It works just fine. We have a signaling system in place. It's better than actually talking just in case anyone other than HQ is listening."

Charlie rapidly depressed the call button and then waited for a reply. Someone on the HQ side responded with the exact sequence of sounds.

"That's cool!" said Scott.

"We should be good to go now. They'll be looking for us to approach from the south," said Charlie.

~ ~ ~

The Archers were situated in a rustic cabin building called Meadow. Each cabin around the camp had a different name. Their cabin contained four bunk beds and one single bed placed to the rear of the cabin. The cabin, along with four others just like it, had sat unused until they arrived. Jane was surprised to see that HQ did not contain as many people as she would have thought. By her estimation, there were probably twenty police officers and their families. Plus another thirty people, including some of the children whose parents had not made it to them yet. Jane knew that many of those kids would likely never see their parents again.

"I'm going to head down to the lake to clean up," said Lea.

"Okay. Just stay where you can be seen," said Sam, to Lea's retreating figure.

"This place is great. I'm just surprised that there aren't more people here," said Jane.

"Me too. Didn't the chief say that around thirty officers left this morning for Doris's house?"

"That must be what it is. Most of them aren't here. The place just seems emptier than I imagined."

She went to Sam, holding him tightly. They'd had no privacy since being reunited with Lea. Holding him, Jane leaned in and gave an almost imperceptible sigh of relief.

"What's on your mind?" he asked.

"I'm relieved to be alone with you, and to be here. Finally I feel like there's some purpose and direction for us. Fleeing the unit so quickly sort of threw me for a loop."

"Me too. All I keep thinking was that I planned for everything and still failed."

"You didn't fail. Not even close. This is the nature of disaster planning. Besides, we still have everything you stocked for us. That's an epic win in my book."

"Let's just hope Tank and his merry band of idiots didn't find it."

"They were just opening and looking. I didn't see any real effort being made to dig through the units. They'll meet your wall of junk and leave," said Jane.

"If they don't try to burn the whole place down. Never know with those idiots."

"Hey, Mom! Dad! Look who just rolled in!" yelled Lea from the distance.

Jane and Sam separated with a quick kiss. Jane could barely pull herself away from Sam's warm embrace. They would have to find a secluded spot for some alone time once they got cleaned up. She stepped out of the cabin, looking around the camp.

"Charlie!"

Jane ran toward Charlie, the cabin's screen door banging behind her.

"Jane! Sam! I didn't think you would be here yet. I assumed you would lie low at the unit for at least another day or so," said Charlie.

"We were sort of forced out. Tank and his men found us," said Jane.

"Holy shit. How?"

"We're not sure, but they were cracking open units. We scrambled to leave before they got to ours. Hopefully, if they open it, they'll be fooled by Sam's wall of trash," said Jane.

"Let's hope so. Have you seen Gayle Jones? I'm not sure if you know her. She's my girlfriend. An officer with Porter's PD. She was one of the first officers I put on the trail. She should be around here somewhere," said Charlie.

"Are you sure she should be here? I think she's the officer chief mentioned that's heading up the team of veterans in Porter," said Sam, turning to Jane. "Right?"

Jane nodded as the color drained from Charlie's face. Her friend started to sway; Sam quickly rushed in to steady him.

"Sit down, man," said Sam.

Her husband led Charlie by the elbow to the steps of the cabin.

"I need to find the chief and figure out what happened. I put her on the trail. She was supposed to be up here waiting for me after I moved the last officer out of Porter. Damn it. She mentioned wanting to form up the veterans. I didn't think she meant she would do it herself."

Charlie sat for a moment on the steps. Jane glanced at Sam, meeting his eyes. She worried for Charlie.

Slapping his hands on his lap, Charlie stood up abruptly. "I need to find the chief. Good seeing you guys."

"You sure you can stand?" said Sam.

"I'm fine. Just wasn't expecting this little twist."

He jogged away quickly back to the main lodge.

Jane shook her head. "Honestly, I didn't even know he had a girlfriend. I feel like such an ass. He helped us and we never even asked about him. I just assumed he was alone," said Jane.

"He'll get it sorted out. Let's see if they need us to do anything," said Sam as he took Jane's hand. They walked silently toward the center of camp.

Chapter Nineteen

Travis drove the old Chevy Impala back toward the house claimed by the cops. If he did this right, he would come out of this alive, with a chance to move up to the Boss's second-in-command position. Then all of these assholes would have to respect him.

Although he knew roughly where the house sat, it was hard to find the driveway entrance in the pitch dark of a cloudy night. He counted on seeing some sort of marking that would jog his memory, but so far, nothing had jumped out at him. Not finding the house for tonight's raid would ensure his permanent place at the bottom of the pack, if not a bullet to the head. He needed to find the house and recapture it. Slowing to look at the first driveway along the road, he didn't see a mailbox. He thought he recalled there being a mailbox at the beginning of the driveway. Now he wasn't so sure.

"What the fuck? How much longer? My nuts are getting numb sitting back here all crammed in," shouted a thickly muscled, heavily tattooed moron named Vox.

"It should be right around here," said Travis.

"Should be?" Vox grunted. "You mean you ain't sure?"

"I'm sure. I think. I mean, the entrance has to be right around here. I can't see shit!"

"You don't sound so sure," said Vox.

Travis stopped the car. "That's gotta be it!"

The entrance had no mailbox or sign of any kind. He could have sworn there was a mailbox there this afternoon. Nonetheless, he figured he should get the guys out of the car before they started to turn on him.

He didn't maneuver the car onto the driveway. Instead, he pulled up along the side of the road and killed the lights. The second and then third car pulled up behind him. Just as he was about to get out and address his soldiers, the guys in the third car sprinted past them, headed down the dirt driveway, in the direction of the house. Stupid idiots. He knew what they were doing. Chico, the driver of the third car, wanted to claim this victory for himself. *Dumb ass.*

"Chico! What the fuck? Where's he going?" asked Vox.

"Gonna get himself and everyone else killed," said Travis. "Keep your eyes open and your mouths shut. We don't know what those fools are doing."

The group walked silently down the dirt path. None of them had thought to bring flashlights, making their progress slow in the darkness. Probably better that way, thought Travis. The lights would give them away. Travis could hear the men from the third car up ahead, talking like they were headed to a Fourth of July picnic. Idiots. He was glad they went ahead. Let them get shot first. Maybe it would distract the cops long enough for Travis's group to sneak around the side.

"Okay. Let's stop here. The house should be just a little further," said Travis.

"Why are we stopping?"

"We need to move slowly and figure out where the cops are."

Hearing nothing but the fools in front of them, Travis and his heavily armed crew walked slowly and quietly toward the house.

~ ~ ~

Dale Spencer sat with Jason Donnelly, Howard Pritty and a few others around the campfire. They'd managed to bury the bodies of their slain fellow officers. Large stones and a makeshift wooden cross marked each grave. Spencer had recorded who was in each grave so the families could retrieve them later. The New Order bodies were arranged in a long shallow grave topped by fallen trees to discourage scavengers.

The team had had a long hard day. Fortunately, the farm afforded them the luxury of fresh water, fruits and vegetables. Everyone ate their fill before drifting to their bunk areas for rest. He stayed outside with his radiomen and the last remaining officers, waiting for midnight.

Spencer wondered if he had enough personnel to effectively guard the perimeter. The farm was vast, with long borders. Officers were placed near the entrance to the road and on both the northbound and southbound mouths of the horse trail. He'd scattered a few officers to guard the remaining approaches, which was the best he could do with the limited human resources at his disposal. He hoped it would be enough. All they had to do was listen for out-of-place sounds. Easier said than done by yourself, in the middle of the night, after a long hard day. The team would rotate four hours on and four hours off until reinforcements arrived. He'd tighten the schedule if too many of the sentries missed their thirty-minute check-ins—a sure sign they had fallen asleep. It would be a grueling, exhausting schedule, but they'd manage. Somehow.

"Sergeant, we're gonna try to reach HQ. It's almost midnight," said Donnelly.

"Alright. Let's see what we can do."

The three moved to the communications shed. A soft glow from the lit candles in the house partially illuminated their walk.

Pritty started up the generator with a roar, cutting through the silence. The noise of the machine reverberated off the trees, echoing back to them.

"If the radio can't reach HQ, the noise from that beast sure as shit will," said Spencer to Donnelly.

"No kidding. I can't believe she had all this stuff. Her son must've really been into building radios. Did you see the box back there of spare parts? We could build a second one of these babies!" said Donnelly, slapping the top of the radio.

Pritty came in and sat down at his seat. The two were ready to attempt to reach HQ.

"Eagle's Nest, come in," said Pritty into the handset.

"Eagle's Nest, come in. It's Blue Jay. Over."

"This is Eagle's Nest. Come in, Blue Jay," said a faceless voice from HQ.

"Overlook One is secure. We sustained heavy casualties and require immediate medical assistance. Over."

"Roger that, Blue Jay. We'll assemble a team and try to bring more medical supplies to you. Not sure what we'll have to offer. Over."

"Anything would help. We have two officers down with serious injuries."

Just as Pritty finished his report, automatic gunfire echoed through the shed.

"What the hell?" said Spencer, moving into the front room of the shed. Bullets rattled through the shed's wood siding, spraying them with splinters.

"We're under attack! Repeat, we're under attack!" yelled Spencer.

Donnelly joined him at the front door of the shed, both of them sticking their rifles through the opening at the same time. Two New Order men were standing in the front yard. They were blanketing the house with bullets, seemingly on a suicide mission. Spencer released a short burst of suppressed fire, hitting the man closest to the shed. The other man continued undeterred by the fall of his comrade, pausing only to reload his rifle. Another burst of bullets from an unseen officer stopped the second man's rampage.

Tires screeched in the distance. Nothing stirred in the front yard or house. Spencer sprinted from the shed to the backyard.

"Officer Spencer coming through!" he yelled, making sure his approach wasn't mistaken for a hostile attack.

Inside the house, his officers scrambled around, moving away from the windows. Others checked on the two injured men in the living room.

"Casualties?"

"None in here, Sergeant. I think we got lucky this time."

"You might be right. Stay alert. We don't know what may be coming next."

Moving back outside, Spencer met Alice Gleason on the front steps.

"All secure, Sergeant. We caught a bunch of New Order men creeping their way up the driveway. We managed to neutralize most of them, but then those two breached our line. They made a mad dash to the house—guns blazing," Alice said wearily.

"Nice job. Your team saved us. Things could have been a lot worse. Any casualties?"

"None. We're all safe and sound. Rogers and Cleff are grabbing the vehicle the New Order men left behind."

"How many cars were there? Could you tell?"

"We think there were three cars in total, but we weren't sure how many men arrived. There are five KIA on the driveway plus these two," she said, waving her gun in the direction of the dead New Order men.

"How did you manage to see them walking up to the house?"

"Honestly, we didn't, nor did we hear their cars. The driveway is so long, and with this cloud cover, it's damned near impossible to see anything. We got lucky. One of them stopped to light a cigarette."

"I guess cigarettes can kill," smirked Spencer. "Drag the bodies to the New Order gravesite and then rotate in for early relief. I'm sure your team could use the break."

~ ~ ~

Sam held Jane's hand as they listened to the gunshots over the radio. Doris's home had turned into a war zone. Knowing the team had sustained casualties bolstered Sam's desire to help. He needed to get to Doris's house and provide medical assistance to the injured officers.

"Eagle's Nest, this is Blue Jay. All clear. Repeat, all clear. No casualties. We caught a group advancing in the dark."

"Let them know a team will reinforce them tomorrow," said the chief to the radioman.

The chief turned to Charlie. "I need you to assemble a team equipped with medical supplies and ammunition. Get down there ASAP. They need reinforcements. Looks like the New Order is hell-bent on taking that place."

"Will do, Chief. Once I drop off the reinforcement team, I plan to get back into town. The veterans will need the weapons and ammunition I hid behind my house. I'll join them for the push into Porter," said Charlie.

Sam knew Charlie was desperate to be with Gayle. Standing up, Sam interjected, "I'll go too. I was a Fleet Marine Force corpsman. I can help with the injured."

"Sam! We need to talk about this. You can't just go. Didn't you hear? They were under attack," said Jane.

"All the more reason for me to go. I have experience rendering the kind of battlefield medical care they need. I have to do this. You and Lea can stay here. I'll be fine."

"Jane, we could sure use Sam's help," said the chief.

"Then I'll go too. We need to stay together."

"I need you here, with Lea. She needs your protection more than I do. I'll get things stabilized at Doris's house then come back, no problem."

"I need you on watch rotation up here, Jane. Sorry to be selfish, but we're stretched pretty thin. Most of the team went to Doris's house. Making a big push into Porter leaves us a little exposed up here," said the chief.

"Alright. I'll stay."

"Then it's settled. We'll move out before daybreak," said Charlie.

Sam and Jane walked silently toward their cabin. Holding her hand, Sam stopped and said, "Let's not go back yet. I want to be alone with you for just a little while."

He pulled her close and kissed her passionately and longingly. Running his hands over her body, he felt her smooth curves.

"I love you, you know," he said.

"I know. I just wish you weren't so damned useful. If you didn't know how to patch people up, I would be able to keep you for myself."

Laughing, Sam stroked her hair. "Yeah. But if I wasn't so useful, you might not have kept me around for so long."

"Good point." Jane swatted Sam's backside and said, "Let's get you inside so you can rest up for tomorrow. You're going to need all the energy you can get to keep up with Charlie. He seemed pretty eager to reunite with Gayle."

"I can't blame him," said Sam, kissing Jane one more time.

They walked into the cabin, where Lea peacefully slept.

Chapter Twenty

Charlie kept the team's pace brisk as they moved their way back down the trail to Doris's house. He had been up and down the trail so many times, it was becoming second nature to him. Thoughts of Gayle swirled in his head as he tried to stay focused on the path and getting to the safe house in one piece.

"We're roughly thirty minutes out, give or take," said Charlie to the men.

"Do we know the severity of the casualties?" asked Sam.

"Not yet. I only know that two men need critical care and about six others need the basics. It could've been a lot worse."

"The sooner we rid our towns of the New Order, the better. Things are going to be tough enough moving forward," said Sam.

Sam was right. The New Order was only one part of a long line of problems they all faced. They still had no idea what had killed the cars and the electricity, or how long the grid would remain down. He guessed it would be a very long time, which meant they had a lot of work ahead of them. Work they couldn't accomplish with a bunch of convicts running around the surrounding towns.

As the team made their way along the trail, Charlie caught partial glimpses of Doris's white house in the distance. He could not believe he was once again heading into Porter. At this point, he assumed he would have been reunited with Gayle at HQ, planning the attack on Porter.

"Hold up. I need to radio our arrival to Overlook One," said Ray Ross, an Evansville police officer.

Stopping, Charlie realized how distracted he had become. Thoughts of Gayle blocked out his operational sharpness. He needed to stay sharp, or he would never see her again.

Ross pulled out his radio and gave the agreed-upon signal, turning to Charlie a few seconds later.

"All clear. Ready when you are to move out."

Charlie, Sam and the other five men walked out into the open field toward Doris's house. The driveway was littered with shell casings; several dark brown stains marked where someone had fallen. This must have been the scene of the attack last night. Now more than ever he needed to be alert and ready for anything. His life and future with Gayle depended on it.

Chapter Twenty-One

The Boss paced the front porch of his house. He could hardly believe that the cops had bested him again. He needed to do something, fast. He didn't tell the men, but he was pretty sure the cops were building up an attack force at that house on the trail, getting ready to come back into Porter. Why else would they defend the place? That was what he would do. He was sort of surprised that none of his men had figured it out. It seemed obvious to him.

Then again, this wasn't the brightest group out there. He'd keep his thoughts on the matter to himself for now. Many of them would flee if they knew a storm was brewing. There was little loyalty among them. Food, booze and cigarettes were the motivators that kept this changed world running, but once the supplies ran out, the Boss couldn't count on any of them. They'd slip away one by one until he was left with his dick in his hand and nothing else.

By his last estimation, he had roughly fifty to sixty men still with him. Properly using them would be key to keeping the town. Earlier in the day, he'd walked around town with that idiot radioman Brown. They'd set lookouts in strategic locations throughout the downtown. Tall buildings, the church steeple—all designed to give him early warning when the cops arrived. If they spotted the pigs far enough out, he could plan a deadly trap.

More importantly, he prepared for his own possible escape. If things got too far out of control, he planned to leave. There was no way he would allow himself to be captured or killed by the pigs. He was done with prison.

The Boss picked up his dumbbells and started pumping. Working his biceps always calmed his nerves—except that one time. He had been curling some serious iron in the prison yard when one of the Mexicans would not shut the fuck up. On and on the man went, chattering away in Spanish or whatever the fuck they were talking in. The eighty-pound dumbbell crushed the man's skull, finally silencing the yard once and for all, and killing any chance he had of convincing a parole board he was reformed. Small price to pay.

"Hey, Boss!"

Trasher's voice interrupted the fond memory. He'd wanted to crush a few more skulls over the past day or two, but with his numbers dwindling, he resisted the urge.

"Everyone is where you want them to be. We pulled all the ammo and guns from the station and distributed them to the men. Everything except the guns you wanted," said Trasher.

"Bring everything around back!"

Putting down the dumbbell, he knew he needed to be careful about what he told the men regarding the weapons he had saved. If the shit hit the fan and he needed to run, he planned to leave with a carload of firepower. By his estimation, the weapons and ammunition would be more valuable than food. He could start over and build an army from scratch. Real soldiers. Not these prison rejects.

"Put everything in the back of the black SUV!" he shouted to Trasher and Linc.

"Damn, this shit is hot. I could use one of these semis," said Linc, appraising one of the semiautomatic rifles.

"Hands off! All of that shit goes in the SUV!"

The two loaded the SUV until the back end of the vehicle sagged from the weight.

"What're you planning on doing with all this?" asked Trasher.

"It's strategy. We need to be ready for a second fight in a fallback location. These are the weapons we'll use to rearm the troops," said the Boss, trying to appear like a master strategist.

"Shit cool!" said Trasher, hitting Linc's shoulder. "See, I told you the Boss knows what he's doing! Shit cool, man. Shit cool!"

Satisfied that he had everything he needed to get out of town, all he needed to do now was wait. Picking up the dumbbells, he watched his arms as his numerous tattoos moved in pace with each pump.

Chapter Twenty-Two

Brown moved quickly through town. The whole morning had been spent with the Boss, looking for "sniper nests," as the Boss put it. The Boss acted like he was some sort of military mastermind instead of a gangbanger like the rest of them. Having to pretend to support the Boss was getting old.

After the cops had easily defeated two attacks on that house on the trail, the Boss became convinced that it was only a matter of time before the cops moved on the town. Brown figured he was right. He also needed to be sure the cops won. Telling them where the snipers had been positioned would give the cops the advantage they needed.

Brown picked his way through the backyards. He carefully chose his path to stay out of the view of the New Order men. The last thing he needed was one of them catching him with Marta. Knocking on Marta's back door, he waited for her to let him in. They had begun meeting almost every day. Being with Marta made Brown feel like a regular person again, not just an escaped convict.

"Brown! Hurry up before they see you," said Marta when she opened the door.

"I brought you a couple of candy bars and half a bottle of water. It was all I could grab without looking suspicious."

Taking the water first, Marta swallowed the bottle's contents in nearly one gulp.

"Thank you!" she said, wiping her mouth with the back of her hand. "What's going on out there? The New Order guys have been moving around a lot."

Sitting down at her kitchen table, he said, "They're planning to stop an attack by the cops. Last night didn't go well for them. Again. Only a handful of them returned from their little raid," said Brown.

"Damn right! The cops are pushing back. Finally. I feel like we've been waiting forever. Last night I listened to the cops calling HQ. I couldn't hear HQ, but I could hear Doris's radio loud and clear."

"You need to tell them the locations of the New Order men. The Boss has them hidden all over, waiting for them to push into town. They need to be warned, or they'll get cut down before they ever make it inside the town."

"Shit! Okay. I'll do it tonight. I haven't been saying anything on the radio, just listening. After the latest scare, I don't want to be found out."

"You won't. I disabled the radio at the station. They aren't hearing shit."

"How did you manage that?"

"Just yanked out a few wires. They're all too stupid to figure it out," said Brown with a chuckle.

"Alright, I'll radio Doris's house tonight."

"Here, I drew out a rough map of where the guys are hidden. Make sure they know."

"Will do."

Marta opened the wrapper of one of the candy bars and munched on it. Neither moved from the table or said anything. Brown knew he should leave; being gone for too long raised suspicions. However, he couldn't seem to pull away. Being in Marta's house evoked images of happy family meals, movies, bowls of popcorn and love. All things he'd given up when he started running with the wrong crowd. Regret over his past and hope for the future combined to form a potent sense of duty to protect Marta and the cops who would be fighting for their lives.

Chapter Twenty-Three

Sam scrubbed his hands in the washbasin placed on top of Doris's living room bureau. Looking around the room, he could hardly believe this was the same pleasant, cheery home he'd visited only a few days ago. Officers from Porter and Evansville came and went in a near constant buzz of activity. The injured and wounded lay on the couches or floor, waiting for assistance.

Two of the men were seriously injured. Sam had managed to remove a bullet from Deputy Sinclair's shoulder. With a few days' rest, the proper antibiotics and a generous amount of painkillers, Sinclair should be able to make a near full recovery. However, their current situation afforded none of those luxuries. Sinclair would be lucky if his wound did not get seriously infected.

"Can I get you more water?" asked Sam, changing the cool cloth on Sinclair's forehead.

"No. I'm good."

"You need to stay hydrated. How about just a little?"

Sam held the glass to the injured man and watched as he weakly sipped.

Turning to Jordan Avery, Sam said, "How're you holding up?"

"I feel like a piece of Swiss cheese."

"Here, these should help." Sam held a glass of water for the man while he washed down the four aspirin he had offered.

Sam knew that aspirin was hardly enough to cut the pain, but it was all he had. Avery's injuries were more substantial than he could handle with the limited resources at his disposal.

"Close your eyes. Try to get some rest," he told the man, covering him with a blanket.

Avery was shivering in the stifling heat. Sam knew he needed to get the man to a hospital, or they would soon bury another Porter police officer. Voices from the kitchen drew Sam's attention away from the men. Charlie, Dale Spencer and Mark were all sitting at the kitchen table, discussing the plans to push into Porter.

"My house is here. I hid my entire collection of weapons and ammo in a shallow cave right on my property," said Charlie, pointing to a map. "I need to grab everything and then meet up with the veterans."

"How long will it take you to get to your house on foot?" asked Spencer.

"At a good clip, not more than five to six hours. The tricky part will be carrying everything to their location. I have several heavy bags loaded with the weapons and ammo. I can barely carry one bag myself, let alone the rest of them."

Sam sat next to Mark at the kitchen table, surveying the map. "Where are the veterans?"

Pointing to the map, Spencer said, "They're at a hunting lodge approximately here."

"Looks like a full day hike to get from your house to the hunting lodge," said Sam, turning to Charlie. "Maybe longer carrying one of those bags."

"That's what I'm thinking. I'll have to spread the walk over two days."

"You'll need to avoid these areas," said Sam, pointing to the map. "I recommend you make a wide arc around the town. It'll add distance, but you should mostly avoid the New Order."

"I'll go with you," said Mark, causing all of them to turn in his direction.

"You sure?"

"I'm sure. I'm a veteran too. I need to be with those guys."

"Thanks. I could sure use your help. We'll leave before sunrise."

Charlie and Mark left the table, heading outside with the others.

"Gotta sec?" Sam asked Spencer.

"Sure, what's up?"

"We need to get Avery and Sinclair to a hospital. I managed to get the bullet and most of the fragments out of Sinclair's shoulder, but Avery's injuries are beyond my abilities. Both require immediate assistance."

"How long do you think they can wait?"

"Avery needs to be seen now. Sinclair can likely wait until tomorrow. Possibly longer. But I would rather not chance it. If an infection sets in, he's in serious trouble. What's the status of the Chase Memorial Hospital?"

"Last I heard, Memorial was being held by its security officers and a few cops. Apparently, the New Order tried to hit it right away, but they were held off and haven't been back yet. The cops were able to secure the building fairly quickly. I think a family member of a Porter officer happened to be recovering at the hospital when the shit hit the fan. The first thing he did was hightail it to the hospital, lock it down and wait for the New Order. Without his efforts, the hospital would have been gutted. I think one or two other officers from Porter followed him, but I'm not sure."

"We need to use a vehicle to get Avery and Sinclair to the hospital."

"Okay, let me see what I can do. We have three cars, courtesy of the New Order. We might be able to drive them to the hospital and get back without being spotted. Last thing we want is more attention drawn to this location."

"I'll do what I can to prepare them for transport. It won't be an easy ride for either of them," said Sam, getting up from the table.

Chapter Twenty-Four

Marta paced the rooms of her dark house. The nights were the worst for her. She rationed her limited candles and batteries, allowing only the slightest light at night. Being alone in the dark with the New Order men roaming the streets terrified Marta. Bad things always seemed to happen at night. The guys would get drunk and rip people from their homes. Often the nights were filled with the screams of sorrow from her neighbors.

She had once loved her home. The lovingly restored old Victorian had been her home for more than twenty years. Lately, her home had become a prison. Venturing outside was not an option. She needed to stay hidden from the men. During the day, she chanced opening a few windows, but at night she shut the place tight, hoping to remain off their radar.

Walking the steps to the third floor, Marta wondered how much longer the radio's battery would last. Turning the dials, the radio powered again. One of these days it wouldn't. Relieved, Marta called out into the night.

"Blue Jay, come in. Blue Jay, come in."

"This is Blue Jay. Come in."

"It's Marta, um, I mean Overlook One."

Balancing the obvious necessity for radio secrecy with the need to warn the police of the sniper locations, Marta hesitated.

"All secure here. What's your status?"

"Secure here. Have a treasure map for you. Over," she said.

She waited, hoping the police on the receiving end of her communication understood her message.

"Roger that. Pizza delivery tomorrow, late day."

"Perfect! I mean roger. Over."

"Blue Jay out."

Turning off the radio, Marta looked out the window across the dark town. The crescent moon lit the night in a shadowy silver glow. For the first time in weeks, Marta felt a glimmer of hope. Delivering the map with the locations of the snipers would give the police a tremendous advantage in the coming fight. Marta swelled with pride.

~ ~ ~

Donnelly and Pritty adjusted the dials on the radio, attempting to clear the signal to the HQ. Sam listened to the entire exchange between Marta and Pritty, wondering if Jane and Lea heard the same communication.

"What do you think she meant by a treasure map?" he asked Charlie.

"Hard to say. Maybe the vets have relocated, or the New Order fanned out in a different direction," offered Spencer.

"I guess we'll find out tomorrow."

"Eagle's Nest, this is Blue Jay. Come in," said Pritty.

"Blue Jay, this is Eagle's Nest. Over."

"All secure at Blue Jay. Over."

"Eagle's Nest is secure. What is the status of the injured? Over."

"Two require immediate transport to Memorial in the morning. Over."

"Roger that. Out."

Pritty turned off the radio.

"I'll get the generator," said Sam, heading out of the shed.

He knew they had to maintain radio silence outside of necessary communications, but he would have liked to let Jane know he was okay, in case she was listening. His inability to communicate with her bothered him more than he imagined it would. Being away from his family after the events of the last few days had begun to take its toll. Turning off the generator, Sam made his way inside Doris's house. He slept on the floor in the living room, near the injured men. The sound of Avery's raspy breathing worried Sam. He reconsidered his plan to hold back on using the few doses of antibiotics he carried in his bag.

The hasty retreat from the storage unit only afforded Sam enough time to grab a very basic field medical pack, with a few backup items. Seeing the number of injured people at Doris's house reminded Sam how quickly things could deteriorate for everyone. If the New Order managed to get into the unit and steal all of their supplies, the items in his medkit represented everything he possessed to keep his family healthy.

The limited antibiotics he carried would be depleted in a matter of hours if he used them to treat the officers. The use of those pills would barely put a dent in the need here at Doris's house and likely not save Avery. He carried a few doses of a broad antibiotic more typically used to treat ear or sinus infections. Saving these for his family suddenly seemed like a better use of his limited resources.

Selfishness did not sit well with Sam. Turning on his side, Sam tried to sleep, Avery's laborious breathing a constant reminder of the tough decision.

~ ~ ~

Jane walked up to the dark cabin, the glow of the moonlight illuminating her path. Lea sat on the cabin step.

"Did you hear anything about Daddy?"

"I didn't get to talk to him, but they said Doris's house is secure."

"Secure? What does that even mean? Nothing is secure." Lea's voice rose as she spoke.

"Keep your voice down. People are trying to sleep."

"Sorry. I'm worried about him. Why did he have to go? This is ridiculous. We should all be together."

"They need his medical expertise."

"Then we should have gone too."

"You see this place. There's hardly anyone here to guard the HQ. I'm needed here and he's needed there. End of story."

Jane didn't want to argue with Lea. She knew their daughter was worried, and so was she. There just was no point going over a decision that had been made.

Taking a seat next to Lea on the step, she said, "Come on. Let's rest. There's nothing we can do sitting here worrying like a couple of sailors' wives."

Lea chuckled at the reference and said, "I know you're right. I'm just scared for him."

"Me too, sweetie. Me too," said Jane, stroking her daughter's hair.

Jane purposely omitted the part about the medical transfer to Memorial. She knew driving a vehicle across town could go south quickly. The only cars on the road were New Order. The sound of a lone vehicle would draw the attention of every New Order crazy in the area. She tossed and turned on her bunk, hoping Sam realized how dangerous the transport would be. Frustration at not being able to talk to him and fear for his safety consumed her.

Chapter Twenty-Five

Sam did the best he could to prepare the injured men for transport. All he could do for them was pack their wounds well enough to stop, or at least slow, any bleeding. Avery's abdomen wound would not stop seeping. He knew a bullet must have nicked one or more of the man's internal organs. Knowing that nothing in his field kit would have helped them made Sam feel a little better about his decision to withhold their limited supply of medicines. Avery needed surgery above all, which he'd arranged.

"They ready to go?" asked Spencer.

"As ready as they can be. I'll need a hand getting them to the car. I created two makeshift stretchers," said Sam.

"Alright. We put the seats down in the SUV. They should fit in the back."

"That works. I'll sit back there with them, somehow."

"No way. I can't let you ride in the truck too. I need every inch of that SUV for mission-capable personnel. They'll be moving fast and traveling hot. I need people who can shoot hanging off the sides or from the limited space inside."

"Sergeant! We're ready to go!" said one of the men from the front porch.

"All right, we need a hand moving these two!" yelled Spencer.

Several officers came into the house and carried the two men away. It wasn't the smoothest transition, but under the circumstances, they did a fine job. The men were loaded into the back of the dusty SUV, with just enough room to shut the rear cargo hatch. Two armed officers stood outside on the running boards, one on each side, holding onto the rooftop cargo rack. Another sat in the passenger seat and a fourth sat squeezed between the two stretchers, his rifle protruding from the missing back window. The truck looked loaded and ready for action. A crude white flag with a red cross was taped to the antenna.

"Do you think the flag will be enough to alert the hospital personnel that this isn't another New Order attack?" Sam asked Spencer.

"Let's hope so. I'm not sure why their comms aren't working. You would think with the large hospital generators, they'd be all set to communicate."

"Are you going to supply a radio?"

"Two. I'm hoping to hear back from the team this afternoon." Spencer walked toward the driver's side window and said, "Good luck and Godspeed." He patted the side of the truck and moved out of the way.

Sam and Spencer stood side by side, watching the brave men and women heading out into an uncertain fate.

Chapter Twenty-Six

Charlie and Mark made excellent time getting to Porter, thanks to Mark's prime physical condition. Finally, he was able to move at a pace more suitable for the situation. He could tell Mark felt the same way. Running on the horse trail felt good.

"Hey, let's hold up. We're almost there. The New Order seemed pretty keen on taking Doris's house. They might have set up shop at my place after discovering the horse trail."

"You got it."

Mark slowed and then stopped, dropping his light pack to the ground. Neither man packed much beyond water and a day's supply of food. They needed to reserve their strength for carrying Charlie's stash. Looking through binoculars, Charlie surveyed his land and house from a safe distance. Through the trees, the house looked still. No signs of the New Order men.

"Looks quiet. Let's take a moment to make sure," said Charlie.

Mark crouched behind a thick, fallen tree and aimed his scoped rifle toward the house, slowly panning left and right. Charlie carefully searched the property, looking for anything out of place. After a few minutes, Charlie lowered the binoculars.

"What do you think?" said Charlie.

"Looks abandoned, unless this is the most disciplined group of gangbangers we've come across yet."

"We'll approach cautiously. The bags are around back."

The men moved deliberately, but vigilantly to the hidden cave behind Charlie's house. They dragged the bags out of the cave and lined them up on the ground. He wasn't sure how the hell the two of them were going to manage the two extremely heavy bags, given the distance they needed to travel. They'd have to shuffle things up, maybe put the ammunition in one and spread the rifles between the remaining bags. Charlie glanced at his house for a few seconds, thinking about something inside. Mark jarred him out of his trance.

You want to go in? Have a look around? Seems like no one's here."

"You read my mind. Yeah. I need to grab something. If it's still there."

"I'll watch your back out here."

"Thanks. I'll just be a second."

Charlie ran around the house and into the side door. He needed to quickly find Gayle's engagement ring. When everything started happening, he'd hid it in the pocket of an old shirt in the spare room. Hopefully, the New Order didn't find it too. Last time he was in the house, he was so focused on getting the weapons out quickly that he forgot about the ring. After he had left, he could have kicked himself for leaving it. It was silly to grab the ring, but he knew the ring would make Gayle happy. It was all the hope he could offer her in this grim new world.

Thumbing through the clothes in the closet was quick and easy. Most of the shirts and slacks hanging had been ripped off the hangers and thrown throughout the room. The shirt with the ring was gone. *Damn them.* He quickly clawed through the clothes strewn across the floor, finding the old blue shirt. Somehow, the ring had managed to stay put. He grabbed it and ran to meet Mark.

"Let's rearrange this stuff and get out of here," he said with a renewed spring in his step.

"By the way, nice place," said Mark. "Great property."

"It was until those assholes trashed it."

The two moved their way slowly across the outskirts of Porter, weighed down by the cache of weapons.

Chapter Twenty-Seven

Marta sat at her kitchen table, unsure of what to do. Wringing her hands over and over again, she reviewed the events from last night. She'd told the police that she had a map for them. That was fine. They were coming to grab it. However, the next morning, she looked more closely at the map. One of the sniper nests overlooked her backyard. She had unwittingly invited the officers coming to her home into a trap.

Over and over again, she considered calling back to Doris's house. Daytime communications were risky at best. She knew she shouldn't do it. She also assumed that the radio was turned off during the day to conserve fuel. Trying to reach them during the day could just end up getting her killed. Then again, Brown had said he'd disabled the radio in the police station; maybe she could get away with it. Over and over again she thought through the situation she had created, searching for the best solution.

A soft knock on her back door broke her concentration.

"What are you doing here?" she asked Brown as she opened the door. "Can't they see you? Your map has one of their positions in the old Miller warehouse. Geez, you're gonna get us killed!"

"Don't worry. They're back at the station, eating. Those idiots can't even set up a proper watch schedule. Besides, I just came to bring you these," said Brown, handing her two bottles of water.

The warm bottles of water were pure gold. Dehydration had been the hardest thing about her confinement. Thoughts of drinking water, or anything at all, were a constant companion.

"Holy crap! Thank you!" she said, opening the first bottle hurriedly.

Marta took huge gulps of water.

"Hey, slow down. You might get sick chugging like that!"

"I know. I know. I'm just so damned thirsty. Can you sit for a minute? I think I made a huge mistake. I don't know what to do."

"I can't stay long. They'll be coming back soon."

"Someone is coming here later today to grab the map."

"That's good news. Wait. Shit. They can see the back of your house."

"And I have no way to warn the officer coming here. The radios are off during the day to conserve fuel."

"Fuck me."

"What should I do? They'll walk right into a trap and get killed or captured."

"Only one thing I can do. I'll go and replace Snuff, the guy in the warehouse."

"Can you do that?"

"Only one way to find out," said Brown, standing to leave. "Stay put."

"Thanks, I don't know what I would do without you," said Marta.

Brown slowly closed the door behind him and Marta latched it. Brown had been consistent in his support of the police. Risking his life over and over again for her and the other citizens of Porter. She tried not to worry about what would happen to Brown when the cops recaptured the town.

Chapter Twenty-Eight

Brown swiftly walked through the backyards to get to the warehouse, with the hope of beating Snuff back to the site. The man was dumb as rocks, but he could shoot. Snuff could easily kill anyone coming or going to Marta's house. Brown took the stairs to the office two at a time, arriving at an open door.

"Hello?" he said, sticking his head inside.

The office was empty. Perfect. He set himself up at the window, making sure he had a clear view of Marta's backyard. The view was a little too clear. Snuff would have to be on the toilet to miss the cops.

"Hey, man. What're you doing here?" asked Snuff, barging into the room.

"Thought I would give you a break. Must be boring as shit."

"Don't you need to be at the station, trying to fix that piece of shit radio?"

"Nah. We've done all we can. I can't get the thing to work. Why don't you take a break? I'll stay here the rest of the day."

"I don't need a break, I just got back from lunch. I'll be just fine right here. I sort of like the quiet, just sitting here looking out the window. Downright peaceful."

Brown didn't know what to do. The man clearly would not leave. He had no way to make Snuff go without raising suspicions.

"I'll hang with you, then. Get some of that peace and quiet for myself."

Brown rolled another office chair to a second window. From his vantage point, he could see Marta's house and the road leading out of town.

"Suit yourself, hoss."

The men sat silently looking out the windows. Brown secretly flipped the safety off his weapon, weighing his options.

~ ~ ~

Mark had never spent any time in Porter. As a resident of Evansville, his visits to Porter were only short trips for dinner or shopping. Although he did not know Porter well, he did know they made a wide arch around the town. The two walked through the woods most of the way.

The bags they carried slowed them down considerably. Mark estimated that one of his bags probably weighed at least one hundred and fifty pounds.

Breathing heavily, Mark asked, "How much further until we cut into town?"

"Another thirty minutes at this rate. These bags are a bitch to carry."

"Mine too. But it'll be worth it to have some decent firepower."

"I'm hoping this stash will help to even the playing field against the New Order. All too often the bad guys outgun us. Not this time," Charlie said with obvious pride.

"Judging from the weight of my bags, seems like you could've armed a small country."

"Or an army of veterans," said Charlie. "Once we get to the other side of that outcropping of trees, we should stash these bags. If we get caught, at least the New Order won't get them. Plus, there's no way we can stealthily move around the town with these."

Charlie's words were a grim reminder to the men of the dangerous situation they faced in town.

~ ~ ~

Time dragged by slowly for Brown. Being stuck in the stifling warehouse with Snuff had started to take its toll. Maybe Marta was wrong and the guys weren't coming today? What if he sat here bored out of his skull for nothing? He started to consider calling it quits for the day, leaving Snuff alone. Standing and stretching, Brown weighed his options, becoming more and more convinced that no one would be coming.

"You leaving?"

"I'm thinking about it, unless you want to?" offered Brown.

"Nah, I'm good right here." Snuff leaned back in the office chair, slightly reclining.

"Alright, man, I'm outta here. Catch you on the flip side," said Brown.

Brown left the office, walking down the dark staircase to the street.

"Holy shit! Brown, get up here!" shouted Snuff.

Brown ran back to the office, two steps at a time. Looking across the yards, he saw two armed men moving slowly through the yards toward Marta's house.

"Fuck yeah! We got ourselves two coppers! Look at them, short fucking hair and everything."

Snuff leaned into the window, steadying his weapon on the men. Even if he didn't kill both men, the sound of the gunshots would alert every New Order thug in the area. The place would be crawling with them in no time at all. He needed to act fast. Grabbing a letter opener off a nearby desk, Brown moved to Snuff purposefully. In one swift movement, he jammed the opener into Snuff's neck, ripping open the man's carotid artery.

Snuff immediately dropped his rifle and grabbed his neck with one hand. His other hand pawed helplessly at the windowsill. With stunned eyes, he sank to the floor, staring up at him. Brown picked up Snuff's rifle and waited until the man bled out completely, watching with no sense of remorse. When it was clear that Snuff had been snuffed, he dragged the body to the bathroom and locked it from the inside. He then locked the door to the office and moved down the hall to a second, nearly identical office. Setting up a chair by the window, he hoped no one noticed the change.

~ ~ ~

Marta saw Charlie and the other man coming to her yard long before they reached the patio. Brown must have managed to take care of the sniper at the warehouse.

"Charlie! Hurry up, get inside fast," said Marta, opening the door quickly.

"Marta, you're a sight for sore eyes. This is Mark; he lives in Evansville. How're you holding up?"

"Surviving. Listen. The New Order has men stationed all over town. They're waiting for the cops to come back. The Boss is convinced the cops are planning something and he's getting ready. I have a map identifying each sniper location."

"The Boss?" said Mark.

"That's what they call the guy in charge of the New Order. Tall, super-muscled guy with tattoos all over. Shaved head."

Charlie examined the map, shaking his head and smiling. "Holy shit. How did you get this?"

"Brown, a New Order guy, made it for me. He has been helping all along. He's the one who told me about the raid on your house."

"Are you sure this is accurate? According to the map, there should be a guy in the Miller warehouse. He would have had a clear shot at us in your backyard," said Charlie.

"Maybe the intel is old, or they're changing locations?" said Mark.

"No. Brown went there earlier this morning to neutralize that position. It must've worked."

"Crap. Either it worked or we got lucky coming in. Hard to know," said Charlie, turning to Mark.

"We need to lie low until it's dark. It'll be our safest bet. One wrong step and someone could spot us," said Mark.

"Agreed. Can we crash here until then?"

"Absolutely. Not that you have many other choices," she said.

They all laughed.

"I guess not," said Charlie. "Have you been in contact with the veterans?"

"Yeah. They checked in a couple of days ago. Gayle is down there with them. They're waiting for orders," she said.

"When we leave here, we're going to them—to help coordinate the attack to retake Porter."

"How long until that happens?"

"If all goes right, within the next day or so," said Charlie.

Marta once again considered her friend Brown, unsure of his fate. He would be expected to fight with the New Order. Refusing could get him killed.

Chapter Twenty-Nine

Lea sat on a rock, watching the kids swim. She had been given the job of head babysitter, something she initially despised. She wasn't really into kids, even on a good day. However, in their current circumstances, being around children who would likely never see their families again softened her heart toward them and kids in general. She began to feel very protective of them. Besides, the other jobs weren't great either. Cleaning, cooking and tending the miniscule camp garden were all worse choices as far as she could tell. If she had the choice, she would have requested to stand watch, like her mom.

Her mom had made a point of making sure Lea had self-defense training, knew how to shoot a pistol and a rifle, and could use a knife well enough in close-quarters fighting. Lea felt like she would be able to protect the kids if anyone breached the camp.

Worry over Tank finding the camp consumed her. She could not help but replay images from her past confinement and beatings. Dread and worry over Tank's next move distracted her from paying close attention to the kids at times. She replayed what she would do to Tank if he happened to stroll into the camp. There was no way she would allow him to hurt any of the kids.

She felt frustrated that the chief chose to first fight for Porter instead of Evansville. Even though Lea had not seen much of the New Order's activities in Evansville, she believed that Tank was the only one in charge. She had no idea how many guys were there with him or how loyal they were to Tank. But she suspected that if they eliminated Tank, then his whole posse would fall apart.

When she heard of the chief's decision to retake Porter first, her panic over Tank's roaming freely in Evansville overtook her. She knew he would never stop looking for her. Especially after she'd escaped from him. He would view her escape as a personal affront, punishable in the harshest terms.

She fantasized about fighting Tank. At times she imagined herself winning a fistfight against him. Other times she dreamed of simply smashing the hood of his red Trans Am, his prize possession. She knew neither would ever come to pass, but even imagining a win over Tank made her feel less afraid and more in control. At times when her thoughts became particularly dark, she imagined killing him. However, she knew she needed to let those images go.

Her mom had given her a pistol, a holster and extra ammunition. Everyone was expected to be armed and ready in case of an attack on the HQ. She hoped her skills were enough to protect the kids and her parents. She strongly believed any problems arising from Tank were her fault. Her presence at the camp would be the only reason he would venture into the camp.

Shifting on the rock, Lea stretched her face up to the afternoon sun warming her skin. Splashes of cool water from the lake touched her toes. The more she thought about Tank, the more she wished she could help prevent him from ever coming near the camp.

"Ms. Lea? I have to go to the bathroom," whined a skinny little girl.

"And I'm hungry," complained a blubbery boy.

"All right, let's go up to the lodge. Maybe lunch is ready," she shouted to the kids.

She walked the short distance from the water's edge to the lodge with the six kids in tow. Lunch probably wasn't ready, but sitting down by the water was getting old. She could tell when the kids were starting to get bored.

"Hey, honey!" yelled Jane, coming out of the lodge. "Where're you off to?"

"We thought we'd sit up here and wait for lunch. You?"

"I'm relieving the watch on the south perimeter for the next four hours. I should be back before dinnertime," said Jane.

"You want some help? I'm sure they'll be fine here for a while," said Lea, hopeful for the change in duty.

"We've been over this. The chief really needs you to keep the kids together and safe. I know it may not seem like it, but it's an important job."

"So I've heard. Come on, kids, let's go around back and sit on the deck," said Lea as she gathered the kids. "See ya, Mom."

Lea walked with the little group the rest of the distance to the lodge. Sitting in the shade, they waited for lunch.

Chapter Thirty

Gayle sat at her post near the hunting cabin. The house was little more than a rustic, three-season cabin in the woods, used by one of the veterans for fall hunting trips. She suspected that Bill and his buddies used the cabin as a place to hang out, drink and be guys, away from their wives. It was crudely appointed, showing absolutely no evidence of a woman's touch.

The property surrounding the cabin was mostly forest. A dirt road extended from the house to the small two-lane road that eventually snaked through the landscape, connecting with a main road into town. They felt reasonably confident that the New Order would not be active in the area for a while. Once supplies started to run low, however, the New Order would journey outside Porter's town limits. They might decide to drive down the road to the cabin, stumbling across their location. Hopefully, the town would be back in the citizens' hands before that happened.

Marta had told them that the cops were moving some of their officers from HQ to the first safe house on the horse trail, to set up a staging area for the battle. She hadn't heard how the relocation went, or if Charlie was with them. Saying goodbye to Charlie on the horse trail more than a week ago had broken her heart. She knew she needed to tell him a few white lies in order to stay and help the veterans, but it saddened her nonetheless. Charlie was truly the love of her life. Once they started dating, she knew he was the one.

She and Charlie were supposed to take a trip together right before the lights went out. He had been hinting about getting married. They chatted about where they would live, how many kids they would have, and where they would grow old. She knew it was just a matter of time before he popped the question. Thinking of him made her heart swell, an emotion that was just as quickly replaced by fear. She had no idea where he was or even if he was still alive. Marta had never mentioned him by name. Maybe when they called this evening, Marta would know more.

Checking her watch, she realized that her shift was almost over. She'd have some downtime until the midnight communications window. Josh Simmons whistled as he approached her location. The veterans had worked out a near silent communications system using whistles and bird sounds. If a person did not know what to listen for, the sounds of their communications would imperceptibly mix with the forest's song. She returned the whistle, indicating all clear.

"You ready for a break?" asked Simmons.

"Sure could use one. I'm stiff from sitting here all morning. Nothing has moved, at all. When is your shift over?"

"About eight. Patty is relieving me."

She stood and stretched her body, shaking her limbs loose. Gayle was anxious to leave her post. Sitting for hours alone in the forest sounded like a magical almost meditative retreat, until you actually did it. The boredom quickly moved in, playing tricks with the mind.

The cabin itself was far too small to house the twenty-two veterans who had moved to the location. Everyone had some sort of tent, tarp or garbage bag combination for sleeping accommodations. It was far from comfortable, especially when it rained, but they made it work. Everyone worked tirelessly to improve each resident's situation, sharing supplies and constructing makeshift shelters. The veterans knew what they were doing.

On top of taking care of each other, they immediately formed a rank structure and a duty chart, which included a rotation for the perimeter sentries. They drew a map of the cabin and surrounding areas, making sure everyone understood where they needed to go in case they were attacked. They even started creating long javelin-like spears from sturdy branches cut from the forest. They had plenty of firearms among the cabin members, but taking the town back would require more than the able-bodied veterans assembled around the cabin. They needed to provide any citizens willing to fight with a weapon.

Although she had never been on active duty, her respect for the brave men and women in uniform grew every day she spent with them. Watching the group of relative strangers come together so quickly and efficiently really awed her. The chief thought she was needed to help get them mission capable. However, from what she could tell, they helped her. She had no doubt they would be able to make a huge dent in the New Order's control of their town.

Lying down in her small two-person tent, she tried to drift off for a short late afternoon nap. It was only when she was alone that she allowed herself to relive memories of her and Charlie. Thinking of him always made her smile. Hopefully she would see him again.

Chapter Thirty-One

Tank opened his third warm soda of the day. He guzzled half the can before pausing to let out a long, deep burp. They had moved their headquarters from Lea's house to a restaurant in a fancy, old-as-shit-style house, which had been left empty by its owners. He couldn't remember the term for the style. Old as shit was good enough.

His anger roiled as he thought about how close they must have been to capturing Lea, her cop momma and that simpering father of hers. They'd finally cracked open all of the lockers, finding nothing but a bunch of junk, which was kind of a mystery. Maybe 23C had been their unit after all, and they'd just used it to hide out while they came up with a better hiding place. He'd tried to retrace their steps, but hiking through the forest didn't seem to be getting them anywhere, and it was annoying as all shit. So he decided to take a different approach. Regrouping at the restaurant, he took time to study a map of the area and think through where they could have gone.

The map of Evansville and its surrounding areas lay on the table in front of him. Lake Sparrow sat to the northeast and Lake Juniper was due north of their location. He had never been to Lake Sparrow, but he had been to Lake Juniper. All the kids from Evansville would go up there in the summers to swim, smoke weed and fool around. There was just a bunch of cottages around the lake, a few supply stores and restaurants but nothing more.

Looking at the map, there wasn't much around Lake Sparrow. Looked like a bunch of undeveloped land with rolling hills, a lake and not much more. From what he could tell, there might not even be many houses or other signs of life in that area. Going up there could be a colossal waste of time. Then again, Lea and her family were always going on hiking trips. Her parents were real idiotic nature people. Why anyone would choose to leave the comforts of their home for the great outdoors always perplexed him. Might be worth checking out.

"Hey, Tank, we're all done looking for supplies," said Mac Bower, his second man in charge.

"You get anything?"

"Just some more cans of food, spices and pasta. It's getting harder to get food."

"No shit. And the knuckleheads just keep eating like it was Thanksgiving."

The other men brought several boxes of nonperishable food through the restaurant into the dark kitchen. The light from the wide windows barely penetrated the back room. They would need to open the back door to do any food preparations. Not that opening cold cans of food required much culinary intervention. They'd have to start ranging further to find food. Turning back to the map, he considered their options.

"You still looking at that map?" asked Bower.

Bower and Tank had been friends since grade school. He was the only man Tank would allow to speak freely.

"You ever been up to Lake Sparrow?"

"Just a bunch of nothing up there."

"I'm thinking Lea and her family could be hiding up there."

"How, man? Sleeping under trees?"

"Yeah, sleeping under the fucking trees. I think we should check it out."

"Alright, I'm with you. But let's get supplies first. The guys won't be much use to us if we can't feed them. Some have already started to break off to find their own. Sooner than later, they'll quit coming back."

Glancing at the map again, he made a decision. They would go up to the lake to see what they could grab from the cottages, stores and restaurants in that area. Who knows? Maybe they would get lucky and find Lea and her family hiding out up there like a bunch of frightened squirrels huddling from a fox. Once he found them, he would be absolutely certain they never got away again. Just the thought of having Lea in his clutches again gave Tank a perverted sense of power and control.

"Tomorrow we'll make a run to Lake Juniper. We'll turn the whole place over, grabbing what we can, and then get back."

Satisfied at his decision-making prowess, Tank again leaned back in his chair and guzzled the remaining warm soda straight from the can.

Chapter Thirty-Two

Bruce Sleeper flipped on the switch to the CB radio one of the guys had brought with him to the cabin. The radio was in fine shape, but it was slowly losing battery power, no matter how much they conserved. They needed a charge or it would not last the next few days.

Sleeper had served for eight years as a naval officer; his first assignment was a frigate in Japan, followed by an aircraft carrier out of Norfolk, Virginia. He had decided to transition to the reserves when his second child was born. The long deployments had started taking their toll on his wife, Mary. He was scheduled to do his two weeks of active time in Pensacola when the lights went out. Unsure of what to do, he linked up with the other veterans in town to start figuring out how they could help the rest of the citizens if the power failure was permanent. Given the striking resemblance to an EMP, he guessed the lights would not come on anytime soon. The first thing they did was establish a rank structure. Since Reynolds outranked all of them, as a reserve Navy captain, he naturally assumed control of the group.

When the New Order rolled into town, killing the police and murdering civilians, they knew the time would come when they'd have no choice but to fight alongside the police—to save the town. They just couldn't figure out how to coordinate their efforts with the police. The veterans had no way to contact them directly.

Shortly after they organized themselves at the cabin and started to run out of things to do, Gayle had arrived with two veterans she'd helped escape from town. She filled them in on the status of the police force, or what was left of it. Communications were finally established with the police through Marta. Now he knew they would be involved with the police in fighting the New Order. It was just a matter of time. Until then, he would continue to keep his wife and girls safe at the cabin.

"Sir, are you ready to contact Marta?" asked Simmons, their radioman.

A small group of them stood around him and Simmons inside the rustic camp. Candlelight flickered on the unadorned walls as they all waited to hear from the outside world. Reynolds and Gayle remained in the cabin during their brief calls to Marta.

"Whenever you are," said Sleeper.

Turning on the CB and adjusting the settings, Simmons said, "Overlook One, this is Storm. Come in. Overlook One, this is Storm. You copy? Over."

"This is Overlook One. I hear you loud and clear."

A collective sigh of relief rippled through the room. Sleeper knew how dangerous Marta's situation was. The New Order could find her at any time. If they did, she would be brutally killed for helping the police. Every time they contacted her, he worried that their calls would be answered by silence.

"Storm, you have two friendlies inbound."

"ETA?"

"Tomorrow. Probably later in the day."

"Roger that. Out," said Simmons.

He turned off the dial and turned to the room.

"Who do you think is coming?" asked Sleeper, turning to Reynolds.

"Not sure, but I'm glad for the help. It'd be nice to get more information, too. These calls are necessarily short, but also a little frustrating."

"Last time we spoke to Marta, she said the cops were moving to the first safe house as a staging area. Maybe they're ready to coordinate the attack on Porter."

"If that's the case, we need to fine-tune our preparations," said Reynolds.

Looking over the various noncommissioned officers, he said, "Get your guys to do a full inspection of the weapons, ammunition and handmade implements. I want all the weapons ready for immediate use. Whatever is happening, we need to be ready."

~ ~ ~

Marta turned off the radio. The short communication with the veterans assured her that everything was fine on their end. Turning to Charlie, she could tell he was not satisfied with the brief exchange.

"She never gets on the radio. I'm sure she's there and doing just fine," said Marta to Charlie. She knew her words had little impact on Charlie's state of mind, but she tried.

Still tense, Charlie said, "We've done all we can do for one day. Where do you want us to bunk up?"

"Come on. I have a couple of spare bedrooms. This house has always been way too big for just me."

Marta quickly covered the radio with an old sheet, making it seamlessly blend into the cluttered, packed attic.

"Did you hear something?" asked Mark.

The three stopped in the second-floor hallway and listened. The deep silence of a darkened world answered their query. And then a faintly audible knock came from somewhere downstairs.

"There! That. Did you hear it?" Mark asked.

"I did. Marta, stay here. Come on, Mark, let's go!" whispered Charlie, slinging his weapon to the ready position.

"Hold on, hold on," she said, grabbing Charlie's arm. "It could be my friend Brown. He often visits around this time. I'll go too."

The three walked down the dark stairwell to the first floor, the insistent knocking growing louder.

Peering through the side window, Marta exclaimed, "It's him!"

"Brown, get in here. Geez, we were upstairs. How long were you there?"

"Longer than usual, I thought you might be upstairs, so I waited."

Mark and Charlie emerged from the shadows, approaching Marta and Brown. Brown started to pull his weapon, but eased it back into his waistband, apparently thinking better of it when he saw that Mark and Charlie had rifles pointed at him.

Slapping Brown's back, Marta said, "It's okay, they're my friends. This is Charlie and Mark. Charlie is Evansville PD."

Brown was hesitant, unsure of how to react with the men in her house. He was a convicted felon and part of the New Order. He was also working against the New Order, on the side of the police.

"Relax. They know you're with us," she said.

Extending a hand to Brown, Mark said, "Hey. Thanks for all your help. Marta showed us the map. We basically would've walked into a trap if it hadn't been for you. What happened with the guy in the warehouse?"

"He had a slight accident just as the two of you were slinking around Marta's back door," said Brown. "It was a close call."

"Crap. Do you know if they will replace him or abandon the position?" asked Charlie.

"Oh, they'll replace him. I'm just worried about them finding his dumb ass hidden in a bathroom. Soon as they do, I'm fried. I think I covered my tracks well enough to buy us some time. Guys are slipping away every day."

"You can't go back to them. They'll kill you if they think you've been helping the cops," said Marta.

"I have to agree. If they find the other guy, it will only be a matter of time before they put two and two together," said Charlie.

Turning to Charlie, Mark said, "Maybe he should come with us?"

"No way. I'm not going anywhere. I need to stay here and help. The only way you cops are gonna win this battle is with me helping your asses from the inside. Besides, I need to make sure Ms. Marta is safe and sound. No need to let those assholes get a hold of her. No, thanks, I'm staying put," he said, crossing his arms over his chest defiantly.

"Alright, but when the shit hits the fan, you need to come here and stay put. No one on our side will know you're with us. You could easily get shot. I'll pass your general description and the fact that you'll be here, but beyond that, it'll get too complicated. The chief's orders are to shoot to kill," said Charlie.

"Damn! You guys aren't messing around. I like it," said Brown, chuckling.

"How many guys are part of the New Order in Porter?" asked Mark. "Estimated."

"Probably around fifty, give or take."

"How well armed are they?" asked Mark.

"They have all the police shit plus all the weapons that the cops had in the evidence locker. They've also stripped the civilians clean of their firearms. The guys are very well armed, I'd say. Many of them are even wearing police-issued body armor. They love playing dress up like they're all important and shit. Bunch of stupid gangbangers, if you ask me."

"Brown, tell them about the radio," said Marta.

"Oh yeah, they have the police radio system at the station. It's how I found Marta. I used to listen to you guys talking at night."

"But not anymore?"

"Nope. I had to disable it. The Boss didn't like that I couldn't pick up on any radio traffic, so he put someone in there to babysit me."

"Any chance he will be able to get the radio operational?" asked Charlie.

"No way, the guy is as dumb as a bag of rocks."

"Other than that radio, does the New Order have any way of listening to us communicating?" asked Mark.

"Not as far as I can tell. Those idiots ran the handheld radios dry the first week. The only reason the station's radio is still working is because of the kick-ass generator at the station. Without it, they'd be in the dark."

"That's good news. It means we can communicate during the day. It'll make working with the vets much easier," said Mark, turning to Charlie.

The four of them startled at a knock on the back door of Marta's house.

"You expecting company?" said Charlie, turning to Marta.

"No, but it could be Johnny. He likes to stop in occasionally," she said.

Marta noticed Brown stiffened when she said Johnny liked to stop by.

"I'll go check."

"We're right behind you," said Mark.

Marta took a quick look between the curtains to the backyard before opening the door.

"Johnny!"

"Hey, Marta. I thought I would check in on you."

"It's okay, guys."

Charlie was the first to come out of the shadows. "Johnny! Wow, am I glad to see you. I know it's only been a couple of weeks, but boy, does it seem longer. How have you been holding up?"

"We're okay. I've been trying to steal food from the New Order for grandma, but the lack of food and water is starting to get to her."

Suddenly, Marta felt guilty about the few items Charlie and Mark had brought her.

"Here. Why don't you take these to her? She could probably use them more than me."

"That's really kind of you. Thanks, Marta."

"Hey, Johnny."

"Geez, Brown. You're here too?"

"I was just checking on her."

"Johnny, meet my friend Mark. He lives in Evansville," said Charlie, motioning to Mark.

"Brown, are the guys in their lookout posts right now? Or do they take a break for the night?"

"I don't know, but I suspect they're all getting loaded on the last bit of booze in Porter. That'd be my best guess."

"Mark, we need to get out of here long before the sun rises, that way we're sure no one'll see us leaving town."

"No shit, you guys aren't as stealthy as you think," said Brown.

"You should talk. I saw your sorry ass slinking around heading over here, no problem," said Johnny.

"Oh shit. And here I did my best SEAL Team Six."

Laughing, Marta felt truly safe and in the company of friends for the first time in a very long time. Since her husband's death, she had been reluctant to get close to anyone. Finally, she felt a sense of belonging and the warmth of camaraderie. She knew the situation would change rapidly, but just for a little while longer, she wanted things to stay as they were.

Chapter Thirty-Three

Sam walked out of Doris's house into the dewy quiet morning. The sun was still under the horizon, yet high enough to color the sky with brilliant oranges, pinks and lavender. He loved this time of day the most. Everything seemed possible and new. Gathering kindling for the fire, Sam managed to get the campfire restarted. Luckily, Doris had showed him how to make coffee over the fire pit, using her iron kettle. It was easier than he expected. He only incinerated the first two batches.

Placing the well-water-filled kettle on the hot grates, Sam waited for it to boil. He knew from experience that once the coffee started to brew, people would begin to stir and his morning solitude would end.

Thinking of Jane and Lea, he wondered how they were doing. Last night Sergeant Spencer had their radioman contact HQ. The communication was nothing more than a simple check-in to confirm things were all clear on both sides. He would have liked to grab the radio and speak directly to Jane. Obviously he knew that was not possible. Every officer at Doris's house had left someone behind. Each and every one of them were feeling just the same. Worried about their loved ones, but compelled to fight. The all-clear signal would have to be enough for them until they were back together.

The faint sounds of fast-approaching footfalls alerted Sam to someone's approach. It sounded as though someone was running toward the house from the front driveway. In the distance the faint sound of a vehicle's engine broke the morning silence. Officer Lovell streamed past him, running into the house, her radio cracking to life.

"The SUV is inbound, ETA three minutes," Lovell said to Spencer as Sam walked into the kitchen.

"Any report of their condition?" asked Spencer.

"None."

"Sam, can you make sure you're ready? The team should be fine, based on their check-in last night, but still. We need to be sharp."

"Will do," said Sam, following the others to the front of the house.

Spencer ran around the house, alerting the other officers. Although he believed the vehicle approaching was the men returning from the hospital run, they had no way to be sure this wasn't a trick.

"Look alive, everyone," shouted Spencer.

The black SUV rolled slowly up the gravel drive. Nothing about the SUV gave any impression of a problem. However, the dark-tinted windows prevented the men and women from seeing clearly into the interior of the vehicle. Moving away from the windows, Sam suddenly felt scared that New Order men had packed into the vehicle, ready to pounce on them.

The front door opened and Dave Mann got out, followed by the rest of the group that had departed yesterday.

"Stand down! All clear!" shouted Spencer.

Sam followed Spencer and the others outside to greet the team.

"How is it out there?" asked Spencer.

"Pretty quiet. We really had no issue at all getting to Memorial and back," said Mann. "The streets are deserted. No one is on the move in any way, either on foot or in vehicles. It was sort of eerie to see the streets so quiet."

"I don't suspect things would be so quiet if you had to go through town. Memorial is situated right between Porter and Evansville.

Maybe the New Order hasn't ventured that far?" offered Spencer.

"Maybe. Is that coffee I smell?" said Mann.

"Oh crap! I left it on the fire." Sam ran behind the house to the campfire.

The coffee had boiled over, sputtering from the top. It didn't smell burnt, so he might be able to save it.

"Got enough in there for us?" asked Spencer, with Mann and a few others in tow.

"Of course, grab the mugs from inside. I'm not a barista, but it's caffeinated and it's hot."

"That's all I look for in my coffee," said Mann.

"I can attest to that. I've been on stakeout with him. The man will drink anything." Officer Susan Newman laughed.

Sam poured the piping hot coffee into the mugs and passed them around. One of the men brought water from the well for the second pot.

"Other than being quiet getting to and from Memorial, what's their status?"

"The head hospital administrator, Beth Pulte, was at home when the lights turned off. Apparently, she immediately went to the hospital, just as all staff is required to do in the case of an emergency. However, as an Army brat, she quickly realized something more than just a blown transformer was behind the lights going out. She had the entire facility locked down," said Mann.

"Over the last couple of weeks, they have thwarted attacks, but just barely. The New Order tried to get in but quickly realized they weren't able to very easily. She thinks it's just a matter of time before there's a full-scale attack on the hospital," said Newman, sipping her coffee. "Hey, this stuff isn't bad. Or my standards have been lowered. Either way, it's good, thanks."

"No problem, I'll keep it coming," said Sam with pride.

"Do they have power? What's the status of the patients?" asked Spencer.

Mann and Newman glanced at each other uncomfortably.

"That's the bad news. When the hospital when dark, it was a small but fully functioning facility. The generators immediately kicked in, allowing the surgeries to proceed, the life-support machines to continue humming and all the monitoring equipment to function. As the days went on, with no indication that the power would be restored, the hospital staff needed to make some decisions regarding how to ration the hospital's quickly depleting energy reserves," said Newman.

"That doesn't sound good," said Sam, shaking his head.

"No. It's not. The morgue filled up quickly. The entire place reeks of death. They had to start piling bodies in the back. Animals have ripped the body bags open and picked at the remains. It's really bad," said Mann.

"They always say one of the worst places to be in the case of a disaster is on life support. I guess that's true," said Spencer, shaking his head. "Did you get a sense of their food reserves and how many people are in the facility?"

Newman looked up from the fire and said, "I think they're mostly fine with the food situation. They are rationing, but apparently the hospital had a lot of stored nonperishable food. Water is more of an issue. They're on a well. However, when the power went down, so did the water pumps. They divert power to the pumps once a day to gather water. I guess it's working out okay, but it could definitely be better."

"There has to be at least a couple hundred people at the hospital. Plus, more keep streaming in. Most people regard a hospital as a place of refuge during a disaster. With their towns under attack, many probably figured their best chance was at the hospital," said Mann.

"It can be a place of refuge, depending on the disaster. In this situation, if the lights stay off for much longer, I would not want to be there. Disease will quickly spread through the facility. Even under regular conditions, hospitals have a difficult time keeping a wrap on infectious disease spreading. This will only exacerbate the problem," said Sam.

"At least the people there were mostly safe from the New Order. The rest of us took that hit pretty hard," said Newman.

Sam recalled that a stray New Order bullet had killed Newman's husband one night while they were at home, hiding. New Order men had been in the streets, lighting fires, drinking and shooting their weapons into the night sky. One drunken thug decided to blanket the front of a row of townhouses. A bullet penetrated Newman's townhouse, killing her husband. Again, Sam thought about how fortunate his family had been given the circumstances.

"Has anyone at the hospital heard anything from beyond our towns? Anything about what happened?" asked Spencer.

"They don't know anything more than we do. When they couldn't initially get anyone on the radios, they diverted the energy use to their patients," said Mann.

"Probably the best use of their resources, given how little chatter we've heard," said Spencer.

"We told them about what we're doing and where we're all located. We also explained that everyone maintains radio silence until after midnight for safety and fuel economy. They will be making contact with us tonight after midnight for a simple check-in," said Newman.

"Good job, it'll be nice to keep them in the loop," said Spencer. "How are Sinclair and Avery?"

"Hard to say. I think Sinclair will be okay. But they said Avery needs diagnostics and likely surgery. Two things they're unable to provide," said Mann.

"That's too bad. This situation stinks," said Spencer. "Once we get our towns back, we'll plan to render aid to the hospital. At the very least, we can organize volunteers to bury the dead. It might be all we can do."

"Getting our towns back is a lot. People can't continue to live in fear. Once we're all safe, things will start to feel different for all of us," offered Newman, lightening the mood.

The group sat quietly sipping their coffee by the fire. News from the hospital wasn't exactly what Sam expected. In some ways it was better. At least the New Order hadn't gotten to it. On the other hand, making life-and-death decisions about who would live and who would die solely because of dwindling resources must have been excruciatingly difficult for the hospital personnel. Once again, Sam reflected on his good fortune in having his family intact and healthy. It was only by sheer luck that one of them didn't just happen to be in the hospital during the blackout.

Chapter Thirty-Four

Charlie shifted the heavy black bag on his shoulders for the third time since they'd reclaimed the weapon cache from its hiding spot on the outskirts of town. They'd breezed through the town easily, before any of the New Order men went back to their lookout posts. The remaining hike to the hunting cabin should be fairly uneventful, except for the physical strain of carrying bags loaded with heavy weaponry.

"Hey, man. Can we ease up a little? We've been booking it since we left Marta's house," said Mark, breathing heavily.

"Sure. Sorry. Why don't you set the pace for a while."

Charlie knew his anxiousness to see Gayle fueled the fast pace to the camp. The anticipation of seeing Gayle mounted with every mile they covered. Charlie had no confirmed information regarding her status or current whereabouts. They assumed she was fine and hiding at the camp; however, Marta did not know for sure. For all anyone knew, Gayle had been taken by the New Order when she left him that morning on the horse trail. Doubling back into town would have left her vulnerable to getting caught. Anything could have happened to her.

Worst-case scenarios about Gayle swirled in Charlie's mind, causing him to lose concentration on their route.

"Should we be turning more toward the east or stay due south? I'm not entirely sure where the cabin is. Are you?" asked Mark.

Realizing his mind had been focused on Gayle and not on the walk, Charlie stopped and took out the compass and map.

"You're right, we should be seeing another path off to our left, heading east. That will connect with the road and take us directly to the cabin."

"Any chance we could have passed it? I saw something like that back a ways. It was just a smallish path off the left side of the trail. Maybe we need to double back to be sure?" said Mark.

"We could. It's hard to tell on this map, without the assistance of GPS and road signs. According to this, if we keep going a little further, we'll meet up with the same road. From there we'd need to go just a little further than we would've from the small path. The small path was basically a shortcut."

"I'm good with continuing on this path if you are."

"Works for me."

The two continued in silence. Although Mark never said a word, Charlie knew the man must've been slightly annoyed with him. Charlie needed to get his head out of the clouds and remain focused on getting them to the cabin. Thoughts of Gayle would have to wait until later.

~ ~ ~

Gayle volunteered to take the morning front perimeter watch. Marta did not disclose who was coming, only that there were two people on the way—and they were friendly. Gayle hoped beyond belief that it was Charlie. She hadn't anticipated how hard it would be to be away from him, with no communications and no way of knowing if he was doing okay. If the circumstances weren't so dangerous and tumultuous, she would have had an easier time being apart. The constant worry over Charlie's well-being had started to wear her down, impacting her tactical sharpness. She needed to focus on something else, but pacing back and forth, quietly listening to her surroundings, she couldn't stop thinking about him.

She worried about how things would be between the two of them now that everything had changed and the full scope of her deception was exposed. Lying to Charlie was something she would have preferred to avoid, but there was no way he would have been fine with her serving as the police liaison at the cabin. Instead he would have volunteered to head the team of veterans, just to keep her out of harm's way. She couldn't allow that. If he had spearheaded the veterans' resistance, then the remaining police officers in Porter would have been on their own. He knew the land around the trailhead better than anyone else and had successfully moved dozens of officers to safety by that point. Knowing she did the wrong thing for the right reason gave Gayle a measure of hope that Charlie would see it the same way and forgive her.

Chapter Thirty-Five

Tank knew the drive to Lake Juniper would be boring as shit, and once again he was right. They decided to take two cars. Tank and Bower drove in one car while four of his "soldiers," as he liked to call them, drove in the second car. He knew they needed to conserve fuel, but the thought of driving an hour with those idiots jammed in the car was more than Tank felt he should have to put up with. He needed the occasional break from the men.

His "soldiers" consisted of some of the guys he'd hung with prior to the lights going dark, plus a lot of dudes from the local prison. When the lights first went out and didn't come back on, Tank sensed an opportunity. Apparently others did as well. The so-called "New Order" rolled into town, intent on taking over. Tank had two choices, work with them or fight against them. He chose to work with them, and in exchange, the Boss put him in charge of Evansville.

The New Order men periodically reported back to the Boss regarding the situation in Evansville. They would also divert food and booze for their shit-bird jail buddies back in Porter. Every time they drove off, taking Tank's bounty to Porter, he considered putting an end to the New Order's involvement in Evansville, but he didn't have the numbers to fight the Boss at the moment.

In a way, Tank hoped they didn't find supplies in the area around

Lake Juniper. He knew the New Order men would begin to leave once the supplies ran dry. He wanted them to leave, freeing him from the Boss's clutches. On the other hand, if the New Order guys drove out one day, Tank worried that the ten or so men loyal to him would not be able to continue to control the town. Eventually, the police would see an opportunity to move back into Evansville, putting an end to his glorious reign. No way he could let that happen. For now, he would feed the shit bags and put up with their Boss until a better plan presented itself.

The Lake Juniper sign stood silently welcoming the men to the quaint summer vacation resort area. The town looked very quiet. Tank had expected to see more people in the area, but the place seemed almost as quiet as it would be in the late fall. Stopping at the first variety store on the smallish main strip of town, Tank realized his first impressions were incorrect. There might not be many people in town, but the few around had done some damage. Most of the glass storefronts were shattered; the contents of the stores, mostly gone. The New Order men pulled up next to Tank's car and got out. Looking up and down the small street, Tank considered the options.

"Alright, here's what we do. Bower and I will go through the stores and restaurants on Main Street. The rest of you split up the cottages. Go house by house. If there's so much as one Dorito left in a bag, grab it. We meet back here in two hours."

The men quickly dispersed, running down the street to the tiny rows of neatly spaced summer cottages. Tank knew if there was anything to be found, it would be in town, not the cottages. People only stayed up here for a week or so at a time for summer vacation. The cottages weren't likely to have large stores of canned food, pasta and booze, like a regular home or restaurant.

"Nice job getting rid of the goons. I didn't think they would go for it. Especially Spike. He always likes staying super close so he can report our every move to their Boss," said Bower.

"I didn't think we would get rid of him. He's probably hoping someone's teenage daughter is hiding in one of the houses. Let's get going before they come back. Anything of value we find, we save for ourselves."

"You got that right. Those guys would slit our throats for the last Twinkie crumb."

The two quickly worked their way through the small grocery store. Not much remained in the dark, dusty businesses. Tank assumed that the people who'd fled Evansville likely came here first, emptying the town's supplies.

The first restaurant contained next to nothing. They only found a few jars of pasta sauce, some pickles and a can of beets. The two could barely see anything in the dark buildings, even with flashlights.

"Let's get outta here. Maybe the other place will have more in it," said Tank.

The final restaurant was an old-fashioned country diner, complete with Formica tables and cowboy pictures. The front bank of windows gave them more light for their search. Tank went around the back of the counter, looking for anything of value, while Bower went into the back room.

"Hey, Tank, check it out!" yelled Bower.

The kitchen area of the restaurant was mostly bare. The store closet had been picked clean and the refrigerator contained foul-smelling rotting food. Other than that, there was nothing.

"What is it? You find anything?" said Tank into the darkness. As his eyes adjusted, he had a hard time finding Bower.

"Yeah—over here."

In the corner of the kitchen, behind a long black curtain, sat another storeroom. The dark curtain must have shielded the storeroom from the view of most people coming into the kitchen. Plus, its location, away from the main storeroom and refrigerator, would have made it nearly invisible to anyone doing a quick search in the near pitch darkness.

"Holy shit! Nice!" said Tank.

The small narrow pantry contained floor-to-ceiling cans, jars and various bottles of food.

"Here's what we do. Take a few things to show the guys and then we hide the rest in the trunk. Got it?"

"I'm with you. Do you think we've much time before they get back?" asked Bower.

"It's hard to say, let's just do this as quick as possible. Last thing I want is to share this bounty with those dumb assholes. They'll eat through it in two days, the idiots."

With none of the New Order men in sight, Tank and Bower quickly filled the trunk of Tank's car. Satisfied that they'd managed to pull it off, Tank and Bower waited for the men to return.

"I'm gonna see if any of these cars have gas we can take back," said Bower.

Tank stood in the entryway of the variety store, considering their next move. Considering where to find Lea and her parents. The New Order men started filtering back, one at a time. Their bags looked mostly empty, or maybe they were stashing food too.

"You guys find anything?"

"Not really, the place is dead," said one of the men.

"Same for all these shithole restaurants and stores. Picked clean," said Tank. "Give Bower a hand getting gas. At least we'll be able to get some fuel."

Tank stood on the porch of the restaurant, watching the men syphoning gas from the few cars on the town's main street. A slight breeze carried discarded papers, wrappers and other garbage through the once quaint town. A bright green sheet of paper tumbled past Tank, catching his eye. He picked it up, examining it. It advertised an "Open Day" at Camp Hemlock. Camp Hemlock was a kids' camp located at Lake Sparrow. *So there is more to Lake Sparrow than a bunch of trees.*

A sly smile formed on Tank's face as renewed hope of finding Lea and her parents filled him. They might not be hiding under a tree, like

Bower said, but they could be at a camp. Checking out the camp would be his next move.

Chapter Thirty-Six

The late afternoon sun hung low on the horizon, stretching the forest's shadows. Night was quickly approaching. Charlie knew they needed to find the cabin soon or face the prospect of spending the night on the cold ground. The map and compass helped, but the area was so rural that many of the roads leading off the main well-driven gravel road were unmarked. Most of the residents in the area were locals whose families had lived in the same place for generations. None of them needed the road signs like Charlie and Mark did.

Once again, Charlie could tell Mark was irritated by the situation, but was nice enough to keep it to himself. In truth, Charlie's limits were being tested too. The veterans didn't exactly help them find the cabin. The directions they provided had been sketchy and vague—probably on purpose. The safety of the cabin required their discretion on the radio when they'd told Marta the location. Charlie understood that, but would have liked a little more information.

"Do you think we should keep going in this direction? I feel like we overshot the cabin," said Mark as he placed his bag on the ground.

"I'm not sure. I would have thought we're right on top of it, but there's no indication that a cabin exists here. Better directions would have been nice."

Charlie put the large black weapons bag that he'd hauled from

Porter onto the ground with a heavy thud. His sore shoulders ached from the strain. Looking at the map, Charlie was once again perplexed. They should be able to see something of the cabin, yet there was nothing, just forest on both sides of the road.

"I think—" Charlie started to say.

"Shhh…listen. You hear that?"

Mark stood straight and called out a loud birdlike call into the shadows. From somewhere inside the recesses of the gloomy forest, an exact birdcall echoed Mark.

"We're here," he said.

All at once, three well-armed men emerged from their concealed locations among the trees.

"Charlie?" asked one of them.

"Guilty," said Charlie, raising his hand.

"I'm Mark."

"I'm Sleeper; that's Simmons and Volk. Welcome to Storm."

"Here? We thought we were lost. There's no sign or road, just dense trees lining both sides of the road. How far is it to the cabin?" asked Charlie.

"Sorry about that. We purposely gave you guys the wrong directions just in case anyone else was listening. Last thing we need is to have the New Order show up on our doorstep. We've been at this location all afternoon, waiting for you two ladies to finish your day stroll," said Sleeper, eliciting a round of laughter from Volk and Simmons.

"Nice. I heard your call and knew we were in the right location," said Mark.

"Army?" asked Sleeper.

"No. Marines."

"The cabin is only a half a mile east of this location, but you would've never found us," said Simmons.

"I recognize that voice. Are you the radioman that called Marta last night?" asked Charlie.

"The one and only. I'm a former Navy radioman third class."

The five men picked their way through the dense brush toward the cabin. Finally, Charlie caught glimpses of a clearing and a small rustic cabin. A few people sat around a campfire. Others chatted in small groups.

Seeing a woman standing off in the distance by herself, Charlie's heart skipped a beat. Although her back was to Charlie, he recognized the curvy hips, long legs and the beautiful color of her curly golden hair. Gayle.

"Look what the cat dragged in!" shouted Sleeper.

Charlie's eyes remained fixed on Gayle. He dropped the bag and ran for his one and only. Pulling her into a tight embrace, he breathed in the familiar scent of her skin. Finally, he pulled back from her, cupping her tear-moistened face in his hands.

"Charlie, I'm so sorry..." she tried to say.

"Don't be. I'm proud of you. You're the kick-ass, tough-as-nails woman I came to love, and still love. It was stupid of me to think you'd be content to sit at HQ, waiting for me. I'm the one who's sorry."

Tears streamed down her striking face faster than Charlie could wipe them away with his strong rough hands. He kissed her deeply and let all the worry and strain from their separation wash away.

"Hey, man. Get a room. This is a family establishment!" yelled Reynolds, from the porch of the cabin.

"Bill! Holy shit! I didn't know you'd be down here," said Charlie, breaking away from Gayle.

"This is my hunting cabin. If you had ever taken me up on one of my invites, you'd know that," said Reynolds.

"Now I wish I had. This place is amazing!"

"Thanks. It's been great for hunting, and ironically, hiding from being hunted. Who knew the place would be so handy?"

Reynolds's reference to being hunted brought Charlie's mind back to their current situation. For just one sweet moment, he'd forgotten.

Unzipping his bag, Charlie said, "We brought you some gifts."

Mark joined the men, opening his bags next to Charlie's.

"That should help," said Reynolds, a wide smile on his face.

"We thought so."

"Let's get everything inside," said Reynolds, motioning to the cabin.

The interior of the rustic cabin was everything Charlie imagined. An old plaid couch sat in front of a stone fireplace. A couple of very used chairs were arranged near one of the windows. The shelves of a bookcase held various puzzles, board games and sets of cards.

Charlie pulled out a seat at the simple pine kitchen table. One by one, he removed the weapons they'd brought and placed them on the table side by side. In front of them lay several semiautomatic, military-style rifles, a few bolt-action hunting rifles, a dozen or so pistols and three tactical-style shotguns.

"Divvy up the items as you see fit," said Charlie. "We also dragged along some ammunition and magazines. You'll have to be a bit discreet dividing up the ammunition. We prioritized bringing weapons over ammo."

"Looks like your stuff is chambered in the usual calibers—9mm, .223, .308," said Reynolds. "Ammo won't be a problem. We have plenty of that around here."

"Excellent," said Charlie.

"These weapons are amazing. Where did you get all of them?" asked Simmons.

"It's my private collection. I'm a little into guns."

"A little? For our first date, he took me to the shooting range," said Gayle to a round of laughter.

"Damn right. And the minute I realized you could outshoot me was when I also realized you were the woman for me."

The men dug into the weapons, each choosing one.

"What's the status of the run into Porter? Are the cops ready to hit the New Order? We're getting tired of sitting around here, knowing those assholes are in our town," said Reynolds.

"I'm not sure how much you guys know, so here's the status. The Evansville police chief had most of their cops relocate to a kids' camp near Lake Sparrow. It's just north of Porter and East of Evansville."

Moving the guns and ammo to the side, Reynolds said, "Here, use this." He stretched a map on the table.

"Thanks."

"The HQ is in this location. Although it isn't marked on the map, the old horse trail snakes through the forest in this direction. We have two safe houses, here and here," said Charlie, pointing to the map.

"Let's mark it up. I'll grab a pen," said Reynolds, handing Charlie a pen.

"The chief moved approximately eighteen officers to this location on the trail," said Charlie.

"But the New Order attacked the house, killing four officers and seriously wounding another two," said Mark.

"Damn them," said Gayle. "Who went down?"

"Peterson, Green, Maeve and Kreen. Avery and Sinclair are injured. As far as we know, they were taken to Memorial," said Charlie.

"I'm so sorry. Were you guys there when the house was attacked?" asked Simmons.

"Mark was, and he apparently put an end to the active shooter threat with one well-placed piece of lead." Charlie looked at his new friend with admiration.

"What's the status of the hospital?"

"We don't know," said Mark.

"Do you know how the attack on the town is supposed to go down and what role we should play?" asked Reynolds.

"The chief plans to split the team at the house, one group going south on the trail, a second group arriving by car. He hoped your team could be in position, here. We would then have a three-pronged attack," said Charlie.

"That could work," said Reynolds, considering the marks on the map.

"When the chief made the plan, we didn't yet know that the New Order has men posted all over town in concealed sharpshooter positions. We need to modify the plan or it won't work," said Charlie.

"How do you know about the sharpshooters?" asked Gayle.

"Marta has a man on the New Order side that gave her the information," said Charlie.

"Can we count on it? Or is this some sort of trap?" said Gayle, wary of trusting any New Order man.

"We aren't sure." He drew out a map indicating all the sniper locations. "Apparently, he intervened, neutralizing the sniper in this location just as Mark and I arrived at Marta's back door."

"Or he told you he did that only to win our trust. I don't know. Trusting one of them is something I'm finding hard to do. I'd hate to divert our team to look for nonexistent snipers," said Gayle.

"I agree. I think we should split off into four squads. Two squads will neutralize these sniper locations first, if they exist, and the other two squads will push into town from this direction as the chief planned," said Reynolds, pointing to the map with the sniper locations.

"Hitting those two sniper nests will open up the town for the cops pushing down from the north," said Mark.

"Exactly. Those two locations would help the inbound cops the most, so we'll clear their path; then the two squads can circle back through town, hitting these spots in this order." Reynolds pointed to the map, outlining his plan. "One, two, three. That should clear the southern route for the vets too."

Charlie considered the plan and knew it would work. The anticipation of winning their town back fueled him even after the day's grueling hike.

"Alright, tonight we'll let HQ know the plan and that we're ready when they are to execute it. We'll have to relay the information from Marta to the safe house and then HQ. Your signal isn't great. My guess is that the chief will want to move forward tomorrow morning," said Charlie.

"That should work. We'll take care of sending the information tonight. We'll get the word out so that everyone is ready for action in the morning if the chief green lights the plan," said Reynolds.

Getting up from the table, Charlie asked, "Do you have a well or stream? I need to wash up."

Gayle took his hand and said, "Come on, I'll take you to the stream."

The two walked out of the musty-smelling cabin into the twilight of the forest. Walking hand in hand, Charlie kept looking at Gayle. He knew how fortunate they were to still have each other. Things could have turned out much differently for them. Smiling, he remembered the ring in his pocket.

"What are you smiling about?" she asked.

"You and me."

"Me too," she said, squeezing his hand.

Chapter Thirty-Seven

Bet sat alone in the dim, stiflingly hot communications room at the Porter police station. He had been assigned to this location ever since the Boss made him "help" Brown with the radio. Night and day he and Brown sat together, adjusting dials, getting nothing but static. Bet started wondering about Brown. He wondered how loyal Brown was to the Boss.

Brown had started acting really nervous yesterday and then failed to come to the station. He still wasn't anywhere in sight, even though it was almost midnight. Something had to be up with him. Or maybe he ran away like some of the others. Bet had no intention of running. Where would he go? Back to his mom, in the dingy apartment they shared in the city? She was probably so wasted on meth that she might not even know the lights went out. No. Bet would stay with the Boss—his only real family.

Leaning over the table, he considered the radio again. He had no idea what any of the dials did, but had watched Brown enough to know that he needed to adjust them to look for a clear signal. The problem was that there never was a clear signal. It was almost as if the antenna was broken. Getting up from his chair, he leaned over the table and inspected the wires connected to the radio. Everything looked fine. He must just be getting paranoid. Sitting down, he again tried the dials, getting nothing but static, as usual.

Bored out of his mind, Bet knew he couldn't leave the radio room or the Boss would have a shit fit. But continuing to turn dials and listen to static had a way of making a person bonkers. Leaning back in his chair, he pulled out his lucky quarter and started flipping. Ever since he was a child, he'd always flipped the quarter. He would guess heads or tails and even make bets with himself. The simple act distracted him and calmed his mind, even during his mom's violent fights with her boyfriends.

Flipping the quarter with his thumb and forefinger, the quarter flew into the air just beyond his grasp, landing on the linoleum floor with a soft thump. He quickly grabbed his flashlight and leaned under the table, looking for his lucky quarter. *Wait a minute. What do we have here?* A single thick cord dangled from the back of the desk area, like it had been pulled out of the radio. He quickly grabbed the antenna, snaked it up to the back of the radio system and plugged it in. He swiped his lucky quarter off the floor and kissed it before putting it back in his pocket. Once again, it had brought him luck.

Things sounded different when he adjusted the dials. He could hear some spots that were not just static, but a clear signal. No wonder Brown was acting so funny. He'd probably disabled the radio. Bet determined to stay at least another hour before joining the guys in finishing the booze. He listened intently, finally hearing nameless people communicating through the dark night.

Chapter Thirty-Eight

Jane walked into the shed, anxious for an update from the rest of the team. If all had gone as planned, by this time Mark and Charlie would be with the veterans. The chief had briefed Charlie on the plan of attack so he could coordinate with them. If Charlie and Mark did not make it, they would have to rework the plan to exclude the assistance from the veterans. She also wanted to hear from Sam. Being apart from him under these circumstances became more taxing as time stretched the distance between them.

"Hey, guys," she said to the chief and the two men seated at the radio.

"Jane, you must be exhausted. You don't need to be here; we can fill you in," said Joyce Rolz.

"I'm good. I'm anxious to hear if everything went okay with the hospital run and if Charlie and Mark made it to the vets in one piece."

"I think we're all sitting on the edges of our seats, hoping for the best on both accounts as well," said Joyce.

Jane watched as the two radiomen adjusted the communications rig. Tension over Sam and Charlie mounted as they waited until just after midnight to call out into the darkness.

"It's twelve fifteen. Anytime you're ready, you may proceed," said the chief.

"Blue Jay, this is Eagle's Nest. Over."

150

"Blue Jay, this is Eagle's Nest. Over."

"This is Blue Jay. Come in Eagle's Nest. Over," responded a man from Doris's house.

"Status report?"

"The hospital run was a success. No information yet from Overlook One. We're still waiting for her check-in. Over."

"Let them know they should contact us once they have a complete status report. We'll be on again at twelve thirty. I don't want to run the radio any longer; we need to reserve our fuel," said the chief.

"Blue Jay, check in again at twelve thirty with full status report," said the chief's radioman.

"Twelve-thirty check-in, roger that. Blue Jay out."

The radioman put down the receiver and turned off the radio.

"All we can do is wait," said the chief. "If everyone is in place, I'd like to commence the operation tomorrow morning. There's no reason to delay. Once the New Order starts to run out of food, they'll expand their range further out. The last thing I want is for this scourge to spread to other towns. I'm sure people are dealing with enough; the last thing anyone else needs is a visit from the New Order."

"Amen to that, Chief," said Joyce.

"Assuming we're moving forward tomorrow, Jane, I'd like you to move down to Doris's house. They're cut as thin as possible. I don't want to leave them wide open to a counterattack while most of our guys are in Porter. I would like you to head up the squad that stays behind at Doris's house. We need to hold that location, even with a reduced presence."

"Yes, sir. I'll be ready to go before sunrise. I should be able to get there mid to late day," said Jane.

"We have two bikes left; I'd like you and Rapp to ride down there as fast as possible."

"Yes, sir."

Jane stood still, stunned by the chief's orders. She had not anticipated being in the middle of a gun battle. Nor did she want to leave Lea behind. The HQ seemed safe enough, but Jane knew that the safety offered by the HQ was just a thin veneer over a dangerous world. The world as they knew it was no longer safe, for anyone. Keeping her family together once again rose to the forefront of Jane's concerns. Maybe Sam was right; maybe coming to HQ was a mistake. What would happen to Lea if she or Sam or both were killed.

Joyce put her arm around Jane and whispered, "Don't worry. Lea will be fine."

"Am I that transparent?"

"Just a little. You turned white as soon as the chief gave you the order. I'm a mom too. I get it. She's safe here at HQ. There're plenty of people watching over her. It'll be okay. You and Sam will be back in a matter of days. And I'll keep her close to me."

"Thanks, Joyce," said Jane, smiling slightly.

She could not shake the overall sense of foreboding. Somehow she knew she shouldn't leave Lea alone. But there was no way she could use family as an excuse in their current circumstances. Everyone had family to protect. Everyone wanted to be safe. It was only if they all worked together that things would get better. She knew she had to go. Breaking the news to Lea would be excruciating.

~ ~ ~

Marta and Brown sat in her attic, chatting until it was time to call the veterans. The two had become close in a short period of time. She never asked Brown what he'd done to land in PrisCorp. In the beginning, it mattered to her because she hadn't felt safe around him. All she could think about was his past. However, as the days went on and he proved his loyalty to the police over and over, worries about his past slowly faded in her thoughts. She knew eventually once everything went back to normal, he would be incarcerated again. On some level, she wished things would drag on as they were, allowing the friendship to continue to blossom.

"Alright, here goes nothing," she said as she turned on the radio.

"Storm, come in. Storm, you there? Over."

"This is Storm, reading you loud and clear."

"Status?"

"The package arrived safe and sound."

Tears pooled in her eyes at the report. There was a tightness and scratchiness to her voice as she said, "Great news!"

"We're ready as directed."

"Okay, I'll pass it along. Over and out."

"Storm out."

"What did he mean they're ready as directed?" Brown asked.

"The chief wants the attack on Porter to go down tomorrow morning. Everyone should be in place by then. Charlie had the plan of attack and is coordinating the vets with the cops heading in. I think you should stay put tomorrow. If all goes well, the streets won't be safe."

"You got that right! Man, will I be glad to get rid of the Boss. They need to know to concentrate on the police department downtown. Those shit bags always hang out there, like it's their clubhouse or something. It's just pathetic."

"Will do. I need to call Doris's house or Blue Jay, I think. Isn't that what they're calling it?"

"I don't know. I thought you were keeping track of all the names," said Brown, chuckling.

Smiling and swatting his arm, she said, "What good are you? Geez."

Turning to the radio again, Marta called out to Doris's house. "Blue Jay? You there? Blue Jay? You there? Over."

"This is Blue Jay. Over."

"Storm is in place and ready as planned. Over," she said.

"Blue Jay is ready as planned too. Over."

"There's a heavy load at Steel and Magnolia. Over," said Marta, hoping they would understand her cryptic message regarding the concentration of New Order at the police station.

"We anticipated it. It's all good on our end. Over."

Relieved, Marta said, "Godspeed. Over and out."

"See you on the bright side, Blue Jay. Over and out."

Turning off the radio, she sat still for a moment. The magnitude of the plan to regain Porter sat heavy with Marta. She knew the cops would be fighting for their lives and for the lives of all the people of Porter. The thought of more officers being killed by the New Order worried her. However, the prospect of the police losing this gun battle terrified her even more.

"Tomorrow morning, you need to be in the basement all day," said Brown.

"And so should you. You can't go out there; you'll get gunned down. The cops have no way of knowing you've been working with us."

"I can't just hide in the basement like a scared little girl."

"Hey, watch it. I'll be in the basement."

"Sorry, but you know what I mean. I should be doing something to help."

"You've done a lot already. We both have. Now we need to sit back and wait for the cops to do their jobs."

"I guess you're right."

There was no way Marta would let her friend go outside tomorrow. If the New Order won, they would all need Brown to help plan a second attack. Besides, she needed Brown.

~ ~ ~

Sam sat in the communications shed at Doris's house. Hearing that Charlie and Mark had both made it to the vets gave the room a certain levity that didn't exist before. Everyone knew that with the help of the vets, they would have a decent chance of winning.

"She didn't mention anything about the package she had for Charlie. What do you suppose happened with that?" asked Donnelly, the radioman, to Sergeant Spencer.

"I was thinking the same thing. Whatever it was, Charlie has it and we have to count on him to know how to handle the situation on that end. It's all we can do. It's twelve thirty; let's call up to HQ to confirm that the teams are ready to proceed in the morning as planned."

"Roger that," said Pritty, picking up the receiver.

"Eagle's Nest, this is Blue Jay. Come in."

"This is Eagle's Nest. Over."

"Status update, all teams ready. It's a go."

"Roger that. We're sending a package to you. Over."

"Does the package change the timing or plan?"

"Not at all. You're clear to proceed. Good luck."

"Blue Jay over and out."

Sam wondered what sort of package the HQ could be sending. The supplies at HQ were thin at best, so he figured they weren't sending food. It was likely more personnel. Despite himself, Sam hoped it was Jane who would emerge from the horse trail.

Chapter Thirty-Nine

Henry Kreen sat in the upstairs bedroom of his house in Porter. Looking out the bedroom window, he waited for his friend Adam Fogel to flash his shades. The two grew up in the houses they now lived in. As kids they would signal each other by opening and closing the shutters of their shades. They'd worked out a complicated communications system that not even the most astute mother could detect.

When the New Order rolled into town, Henry took a chance that his friend Adam would have the same thought. He closed his blinds and started flashing the shutters opened and closed in rapid succession. *Are you there? Adam, you there?* Night after night, he would try with no reply. Then finally, one night Adam answered. *I'm here. Scared and hungry.* Since that night, the two communicated on a daily basis.

Henry knew the New Order had raided Adam's house, along with all the other houses in Porter. He also knew Adam had managed to conceal his hunting rifle. Their houses were downtown, near the police station. The two watched the New Order men coming and going, communicating plans to pick off the men one by one. Even though they knew they were outnumbered and unable to fight, they still planned. It felt good for them to be doing something.

One night, Adam told Henry he had talked to the neighbors on both sides of his house. They were all armed and willing to join the fight. Adam encouraged Henry to talk to his neighbors. Little by little, the men managed to pull together a string of eleven houses all near the police station, all armed and ready to fight. Now they just needed an opportunity.

Flashing his friend, Henry asked, "You okay?"

"Yeah, it's quiet again."

"Better than a fire and shooting," signaled Henry.

"We need a plan to get them."

"I know. If we kill the Boss, what do you think will happen? Maybe we just nail him?"

"I thought so too. But still too risky. We need more people."

"Agreed. Catch you tomorrow."

"Okay," signaled Adam.

Henry closed the shutters and turned in for the night. In the master bedroom, he snuggled close to his wife, Margaret, and their young son. He wondered how eleven regular citizens could take down a gang of hardened convicts.

Chapter Forty

The Boss stood in the parking lot of the police station. On hot, sticky nights, the station was intolerable. Leaning against one of the disabled police cars, he drained the rest of the Chivas from the large bottle. They had emptied every bottle of wine, beer and booze from the houses and restaurants—and still it wasn't enough for them. They drank with the reckless abandon of men who had been locked up, dry and thirsty for a buzz. It was all they knew.

Soon they would have to venture out of Porter to resupply. The question remained if they would all leave Porter or just go to resupply. Or maybe he would leave on his own and never return. He had the back of his truck loaded with weapons, ammo, food and enough alcohol to keep himself busy for a while.

"Hey, Boss! Boss!" yelled Bet as he ran out of the station.

The Boss had made him stay in the radio room until he heard something. The guy did as he was told. He might not be too bright, but he was loyal, and that was something the Boss always recognized.

"What is it, man? You sound like a little bitch screaming like that. Slow down," said the Boss.

"The radio, it was disabled! I fixed it! People were talking! I could hear them!"

"Holy shit! I knew that asshole Brown wasn't doing shit in there! Where is he?"

"I don't know. He hasn't come back since he left this morning."

"Son of a bitch! I want him found!" he said. Pointing to the two men closest to him, he screamed, "Now!"

The men ran off and he returned his attention to Bet. "Who was talking?"

"I couldn't tell, but I think it was the cops! Sounds like they're working some plan."

"What do you mean you couldn't tell? What sort of plan?"

"They were talking in code, using bird names and shit. I have no idea what they were talking about, but it sounds like they're working on something."

"Can you remember anything else? Are they coming here or to Evansville?"

"Sorry, Boss, I really don't know."

"Shit. Okay, get back in there and keep listening."

The Boss stood silently considering their next move. If the cops were coming, they would be ready to fight.

Finally, he turned to Linc and said, "We need to be ready. I want guys watching the trail and the road into town. Give them extra ammo too. And double up the guys in the sniper nests. This is war. We need to be ready to hold our town or go down fighting."

"Fuck yeah, Boss! We'll get 'em. The pigs aren't getting this shit back!" said Linc.

The Boss had every intention of fighting. However, he was also realistic. If the cops turned the tide, he had no intention of getting caught. He would simply drive out of town and start again.

Chapter Forty-One

Jane walked back to the cabin with mixed feelings. She was both excited to see Sam again, but terrified to leave Lea. After everything they had gone through to get Lea back from Tank, it seemed so wrong to leave her, especially considering the fragile state she was in. Lea had suffered an enormous emotional and physical trauma. She needed stability and kindness right now, not a war zone. Leaving her might exacerbate Lea's condition.

She quietly opened the door to the cabin, hoping Lea would be asleep.

"Did you get to talk to Daddy?" said Lea, from the dark interior of the cabin.

"Not exactly, but the hospital run went fine. Other than that, it was just the usual check-in. But I did learn that Charlie and Mark are safe. They made it down past Porter and are with the veterans."

"That's a relief. I was worried about them, especially since they had to go to Marta's house first, wherever that place is."

"I know it was a really dangerous thing they did. Hopefully, it will all help in regaining Porter. Tomorrow they plan to execute the plan to surge into Porter. With any luck, by this time tomorrow night, things will be significantly different for all of us. Getting the New Order out of Porter is the first step of many in getting back home, free of all of them."

"I don't want to go back home, ever. I really don't think I could sleep in that house again."

"I know, honey. We'll figure it out. But first we need to get our towns back."

"Will Daddy come back tomorrow?"

"Actually, about that. The chief asked me to leave early tomorrow morning for Doris's house. I'm going to head down on a bike with Officer Rapp. He knows the way and will get us there quickly. The chief needs me to head up the team that is staying at Doris's house while the others leave for the attack on Porter."

"What? You're leaving? You can't. I need you here."

"I know. I'm not happy about it either, but I've no way of getting out of it. All the cops left family behind to join the fight. At least I'll be at Doris's house and not part of the actual fight in Porter."

"Daddy was right; we should've never come here. We should've taken our chances alone."

"Maybe. But this is where we are and we need to make the best of it. The only way things will get back to normal is if we get rid of the New Order."

"And Tank."

"And Tank," said Jane, brushing hair from Lea's face. "Both Daddy and I should be back in just a couple of days. The time will fly by, especially since you're having so much fun with the kids!" said Jane, smiling.

"Very funny. But you're probably right. They do keep me very busy. However, their constant complaining is enough to drive anyone insane."

"A few more days and we'll all be back together."

Jane used her flashlight to gather her things for the ride out. She and Rapp intended to leave before first light. They had headlamps and flashlights. Hopefully it would be enough illumination for the ride to Doris's house. Jane packed a couple of clean-ish T-shirts and a pair of shorts. They were able to wash their clothes in a basin of sudsy water from the lake. Once dried, the clothes were stiff as cardboard. Not the country freshness she expected.

Lying in bed, she tried to relax into sleep to no avail. Worry over Sam and Lea and the plan to retake Porter consumed her. Being with Sam would alleviate some of her fear. Being in his arms always made her feel safe, warm and happy. She really needed all three right now.

Chapter Forty-Two

Charlie and Gayle lay tangled in each other's arms in Gayle's tent. The sleeping bag and blanket sat discarded at the side of the tent. Charlie inhaled the scent of Gayle's soft curls, drifting in and out of contented sleep.

"I wish you weren't going into Porter tomorrow," she said.

"Right back at you. I don't want you leading a team into Porter. It's going to be extremely dangerous."

"At least I'm not trying to neutralize a sniper's nest."

"I know. The whole thing is crazy. Do you realize that if none of this happened, we would've been getting back from our trip right about now."

"It would've been a really nice trip too. Now I wish we'd bought trip insurance."

Laughing, Charlie flipped her over on her back, kissing her neck. "Good thinking, cuz the insurance companies are probably paying all sorts of claims right about now."

"Oh my, I totally forgot. Yep, I'm the person who tries every light during a blackout."

"You're optimistic. That's why I love you."

Charlie had hidden the ring in a spot near their pillow before Gayle had come in for the night. He knew he needed to propose to her tonight. Anything could happen tomorrow. One or both of them might not survive. At least he would know if she wanted to marry him and she would know his intentions toward her were true. Leaning over, he clasped the ring in his hand and dove in.

"I know this really isn't the most romantic place in the world, but right now, it's the best I can do."

"What are you talking about?"

"Gayle, will you marry me?"

He lifted the ring up to show her. The glimmer of the diamond was barely visible in the darkness. But it was enough to catch her eye.

"Charlie, you're serious…" she said, a little stunned. "I wasn't expecting…I mean, we were supposed to go on the trip…"

"Will you?"

"Yes! Yes! Of course I will! I love you."

"I love you more."

Charlie kissed Gayle with love and relief. He was surprised by how difficult it was to ask her to marry him, and yet, not difficult at all. Excitement over their lives together gave him the additional motivation he needed to make it through tomorrow. Everything would change for them once their towns were secure.

Chapter Forty-Three

Jane wasn't prepared for the difficult trip to Doris's house. In theory it seemed simple. Ride the path due south. No problem. In reality, riding a mountain bike in the pitch dark with only a headlamp was extremely difficult. Her body ached and was covered in bruises from the frequent falls. Ruts and branches obstructed their slow progress.

"You okay back there?" asked Rapp.

"Yep, hanging in there. Riding a bike in the woods in the dark is way harder than I expected."

"We'll be fine. In another thirty minutes or so, the sunrise will start to penetrate the woods."

Glancing at Rapp, Jane knew he was right, but was in no mood to hear cheery optimism. Focusing on the trail, she worked hard at staying on her bike.

~ ~ ~

Dale Spencer surveyed the ten officers standing around him and knew their numbers would be barely enough to retake Porter. The surprise attack by the thugs coming from the trail had put a serious dent in their numbers. They'd have to make it work, there was no choice. With the veterans helping, it might be enough. The last report put the number of New Order men around forty. They were outnumbered. However, Evansville had managed to secure their entire arsenal of riot-control tools, giving them tear gas, flash grenades and other weapons at their disposal. Those weapons should help even the playing field.

"Okay, listen up," Spencer said, getting everyone's attention.

"We have to assume they're waiting for us. We're splitting up into two teams, Alpha and Bravo. Alpha is on bike; Bravo will drive. Each team has a radio."

Spencer squatted and stretched the map on the ground in front of the group. His fellow officers huddled around him.

"We'll drop off Alpha at this location near the horse trail," he said, pointing to the map. "They know about the trail, so we need to assume they're guarding it. Alpha needs to flank the trail and neutralize the men at that location."

The officers on Alpha team nodded their understanding of the plan.

"Bravo, I'll be with you. We'll drive to this location and then fan out on foot. Again, we need to assume they're guarding the road. Once we neutralize those guards, we need to move to the station, here."

"Are our orders the same? Shoot to kill?"

"Yes. This is a war and we need to treat the New Order like enemy combatants."

No one in the group disagreed with the orders or plan. A nervous energy built between them.

"Once we neutralize the guards watching the trailhead and the road, we push to the station. Marta said there's a concentration of men at the station. I want to hit them with flash grenades and tear gas to drive them out. With any luck, the few men scattered around town will either flee or come to the fight at the station. Either way, once we recapture the station, we need to watch our backs until we've gone door-to-door, flushing out any remaining New Order men. The veterans will be backing us up, pushing the New Order men in the direction of the station from the south. Everyone understand the plan and their role?"

"Yes, Sergeant!" said Kara Lovell.

"We leave in five."

The group quickly disbursed. Some grabbed extra water; others made last minute adjustments to their tactical gear. Vests, helmets and shields were loaded into the cars, ready for action.

~ ~ ~

Charlie moved fast through the forest with the veterans. Every man and woman was armed with a motley assortment of homemade weapons, guns and knives. The crew looked a little ragged, but Charlie had no reservations about their capabilities.

The group quickly made it to the outskirts of town. This was the point they needed to split apart, each going to their assigned sniper location.

"Alright, hold up!" he shouted. "We're here. Mark, take your team northeast, starting with the warehouse behind Marta's house. Then you guys will move to the northwest while we hit the nests in the southeast, moving west, like we talked about last night. Gayle, once you get the all clear, your team picks its way toward the station, herding the New Order men toward the center of town. Then guard the road exiting town, for any fleeing New Order men. It's still very early; with any luck, the New Order hasn't positioned their guys in the nests yet and we'll be waiting for them when they show. Let's move out."

Charlie grabbed Gayle's hand, pulled her close to him and quickly kissed her on the cheek.

"Be careful out there," he whispered to her.

"Don't worry about me. We have the easy job. Keep safe. Love you," she whispered.

Letting go of her hand, Charlie quickly caught up with his squad.

Chapter Forty-Four

Charlie led his squad of veterans through the outskirts of town. He was counting on the New Order thugs getting a late start due to the heavy drinking and partying reported by Marta and Brown. His plan was to conceal ambush points outside each nest he'd been assigned, with the hope of gunning down each New Order lookout team as they casually approached the entrance to each structure. The plan would work so long as the men weren't already inside each location, waiting for them.

Charlie wasn't overly confident in his own squad's ability to fight a close-quarters battle against an enemy alerted to their presence. His SWAT experience gave him a leadership advantage, but most of the veterans hadn't served in ground combat roles, which made him very leery about sending them into unfamiliar structures, against unknown threats. This way, when the first team ambushed their quarry, the New Order men would rush hastily to their assigned sniper nests, hopefully making it easier for the veterans to spring their traps.

He moved the group forward in the dim light, careful not to bump into anything that might make noise. He had enough light to see vague outlines, but couldn't make out details. That would change over the next fifteen minutes, and he wanted his people to be in position before that happened.

The first sniper's nest appeared beyond a thick hedgerow, its features barely discernible in the predawn light. It was a two-story house, with open windows facing north, the path of approach for Dale Spencer's police officers. They cut through a few of the thinner parts of the hedgerow and took positions at the side of the house. Charlie signaled for the rest of the squad to wait while he checked out the nest, just in case some of the New Order thugs had decided to sleep in their posts.

He crept into the unlocked back door of the house and silently moved through the first floor, finding no sign of the New Order. Charlie locked and deadbolted the front door, then cautiously moved upstairs, searching each room and finding nothing. This might work.

When he returned to his squad, he positioned two veterans with rifles in concealed positions outside the back door, facing the house. Before he left, he locked the doorknob and pulled the back door shut. If the New Order men tried the front first, they'd find it locked and head around back, where the second locked door would stop them in the crosshairs of a massacre.

He repeated the process for the next four locations. Settling into the low shrubbery next to one of the vets assigned to his team, they waited for the day's events to unfold.

Chapter Forty-Five

Bravo team dropped Kara Lovell and the rest of the small Alpha team on the road near the horse trail. Lovell's eyes adjusted to the dark forest slowly. The sun was peeking up along the horizon but not enough to penetrate the canopy of towering trees along the trail.

The team had a difficult time finding the horse trail in the dark. Their flashlights gave them only mere glimpses of the path to Porter. Finally, once they were sure they were on the horse trail, they picked up their pace considerably.

Holding her fist in the air, Lovell stopped the other four officers.

"Tucker, take your squad to the right; Lutz, we're going to the left. We need to be off the trail."

The team of six split in two and proceeded through the forest, flanking the trail. So far there was no sign of the New Order. Lovell could see glimpses of the town through the trees; she knew they were getting close. Again halting their progress, they hid behind the trees, observing the entrance to the trail. Four heavily armed New Order men stood near the trailhead, chatting.

Lovell knew they had the advantage. The men would not be able to clearly see past the shadowy, dark tree line, but the police could see them. Signaling the other officers, she coordinated the attack on the New Order men, hitting them at once in a smooth, swift volley. She lined up the man facing the forest and took her shot. The loud sounds of her rifle fire in concert with the fire from the other officers echoed off the trees. Two of the New Order men went down almost immediately. The other two men, who were partially obscured from their range, immediately spun around, blanketing the trees with firepower.

The two teams of police took cover behind the thick tree trunks and then returned fire. One more New Order man went down while the other raced behind a parked car. They needed to get him before he got away.

Lovell ran through the forest parallel to the man's concealed location and then boldly darted out of the tree line behind him, firing at close range until the man dropped to the ground.

The other officers ran out from the path, quickly grabbing the New Order's bloody weapons and checking to be sure none of the men survived.

Chapter Forty-Six

Henry Kreen heard the gunfire erupting through the quiet dawn and knew something big was happening. Racing through the house, he grabbed his hunting rifle and a box of ammunition.

"Take Pete and head to the basement! Now!" he shouted at his wife, Margaret.

He watched as his frightened family ran down the stairs and slammed the basement door shut. Getting to his front window, he quickly signaled Adam.

"You hear that?"

"Yeah. What do you think's happening?"

"Not sure, but it sounded like a fight. Not the usual one-sided shooting fest."

"Maybe the cops are back? We need to get everyone ready!" signaled Adam.

"On it."

Henry ran from the front window to the side of the house to signal his next-door neighbor. He and Adam had taught the neighbors a simple version of their code. It was just enough to keep them in silent communication. He flashed Danny, his neighbor to the south, first.

"You there?"

"Yes! What was that?"

"We don't know. Just get ready in case it's the cops. They might need us."

"Okay."

"Start the comms chain."

"Okay."

Henry knew the brevity of their current communications system probably killed Danny. Normally Danny could talk all day, holding up many family dinners with his idle front-yard chatter. Henry had to smile slightly despite the situation.

Running to the other side of the house, Henry quickly signaled the neighbor on his north side. Scott quickly signaled back that the houses north of Henry were all ready for action. Henry knew Scott would be a great asset. Scott was organized and efficient. Plus, like Henry, he had a family to defend.

The neighbors waited in a long deadly row along Magnolia Street. They'd previously decided that all families would wait in their respective basements; each shooter would cover their patch of land and if possible the police station. All knew not to shoot into each other's houses.

More gunfire erupted in the town. Henry could not be sure of its direction. Running to the back of his house, he looked out, trying to acquire more information. He saw two men he knew as local veterans running through the backyards, being led by a man he didn't recognize. The fight was on.

He quickly flashed a message to the others.

"Get ready! The cops and vets are back!"

Chapter Forty-Seven

Bruce Sleeper lay in the bushes behind the old two-story house, listening for any signs of movement. Once Charlie headed off with the rest of the squad, everything had gone dead quiet again. At first the silence didn't bother him, but as the minutes dragged on, the stillness started to work on his nerves. He'd checked the safety on his AR-15 so many times he was starting to forget which position it needed to be in to fire. Then the sounds of distant gunfire rattled his nerves, making him wonder if he should stay in his assigned location or move.

A few of the veterans had brought their own AR-style rifles to the cabin and given the rest of them a thorough re-familiarization of the weapon. Sleeper had fired an M16 a few times in the Navy, which was essentially the same thing, but he'd forgotten most of what he'd learned. The refresher training at the cabin had helped, but he was still second-guessing why they'd chosen him to carry one of Charlie's rifles. At least he wasn't carrying a spear. Larry Goodlaw, the guy lying next to him, was armed with little more than a sharpened stick.

Goodlaw nudged him, drawing his attention to the brightening sky over the trees beyond the house. Sleeper shook his head, understanding his partner's concern. If the attack on this particular nest didn't commence shortly, they might have to find a more concealed ambush position. He raised his head well above the bushes to scout for a better location. No sense waiting until they were fully exposed. The hedgerow separating the backyards on the other side of the yard looked to be a good choice, even though it was further away from the kill zone. Before he could make a decision, more gunfire erupted, this time closer to them.

The rapid crackling of gunshots continued for several seconds, until the town once again quieted. The shots had come from the direction of the trail leading out of Porter, so either the police had been ambushed, or they had gunned their way through whatever guards the New Order had set up on the trail. He probably wouldn't know either way before the fight came to his doorstep.

Yelling erupted beyond the house they were guarding, coming from the street. The sound of footsteps followed. He caught a glimpse of movement in the front yard, but his view beyond the side of the house was limited.

"Who the fuck locked the door?" said a gruff voice from the front of the house.

"I didn't do it. I came out the back," replied another.

"Well, one of you idiots did it! Let's go around the back. Hurry!"

Three figures materialized in the predawn light and ran down the side of the house, oblivious to his presence. He followed them with the red dot sight attached to his rifle, his finger on the trigger, until they stopped at the back door.

"One of you is stupider than fuck," said one of the men, yanking on the doorknob. "It's locked."

Sleeper didn't give any of them a chance to respond. He pressed the trigger repeatedly, moving the illuminated red dot from one figure to the next until all three of them had fallen. He had no idea how many shots he'd fired, so he pressed the magazine release button and dug through his cargo pants pockets for one of three spare magazines he'd been given. Before he could reload, Goodlaw jumped out of the bushes and charged the downed men.

"Larry! What the hell!"

175

He fumbled with the magazine as one of the men on the ground managed to lift himself to a seated position against the house, with a rifle across his lap. Goodlaw reached the New Order thug faster than Sleeper thought possible, kicking the rifle away and jamming the spear into his stomach with two hands. The man gave up a gurgled scream before slumping sideways and collapsing. Goodlaw speared him again, this time eliciting nothing more than a flat groan. When he pulled the bloodied spear back for a third strike, Sleeper jumped up.

"He's dead, Larry! Jesus. He's dead. Grab their weapons."

Gunfire exploded a few houses over, causing them to crouch.

"That's the second nest. We need to secure this house and wait for the police to push through. Then we meet up with Charlie."

Goodlaw said nothing. He just stared into the backyard like he'd seen a ghost.

"You okay?"

"I think so."

Sleeper grabbed the spear from his hand and tossed it onto the grass before holding up one of the rifles for him.

"Let's go. We still have a job to do," said Sleeper, patting him on the back.

Goodlaw nodded and took the rifle, reconnecting to the world and the task at hand.

Chapter Forty-Eight

Mark raced with his team through the backyards to the warehouse. The sound of nearby gunfights echoed all around them. The team got to the warehouse and kicked in the door. The stench of death greeted them. He recalled that Brown had said he'd neutralized the threat in the warehouse. Judging by the strong odor of rotting flesh, Brown hadn't lied to them.

The men quickly moved into the building. Taking the emergency stairwell, the men carefully moved their way up the darkened flights to the third floor. The warehouse was deserted. A line of dried blood pooled from under a locked bathroom door.

"Let's get to the next location. Reacher, you stay here and wait for company. We might've gotten lucky and beat them to their posts."

"You got it. I'll lock the front door and wait by the back side for them to show up."

The men proceeded to walk back down the stairwell, their minds on the next location. Suddenly a bullet ricocheted off the metal handrail from an unseen New Order assailant.

The men sheltered themselves behind the blind sides of the stairwell and then returned fire. The stairwell filled with the deafening sound of their weapons combined with the return fire from the New Order men. Concerned about their ammunition supply, Mark signaled for them to stop shooting. They waited in the darkness. Finally a beam of light appeared at the bottom of the stairwell and then disappeared as the New Order men left the building.

Mark and the others raced down the stairs, taking two at a time.

"Same plan. Reacher, wait for company and then join us at the station."

Silence.

"Reacher!"

The man did not reply. Mark ran up the stairs and found Reacher face up, eyes open, sitting in a pool of his own blood.

"Fuck! Reacher is dead. New plan. The New Order is on the move. Grant, you stay here and watch the street. Make sure to watch your back. They might return. Got it?"

"Got it. I can go between the front and back, watching the streets."

Mark and the other veteran quickly ran out of the building to the next and last sniper location.

Getting to the next nest, Mark called Charlie. "Charlie, what's your status? Over."

"All of our targets are neutralized. What's your status?"

"We lost Reacher, but are holding steady. One more to go."

"Copy that. Let me know when you're done, and I'll tell the cops that they can move into town."

"Roger," said Mark.

Chapter Forty-Nine

Dale Spencer moved his team quickly and efficiently toward the center of town. They hid behind buildings, cars, dumpsters and whatever else they could find. He presumed the gunfire was from Lovell's team but then heard live fire from what seemed like multiple shooter locations. He hoped it was Charlie and Mark with the veterans and not a New Order hit squad going door-to-door.

"Lovell, report your status," he whispered loudly into the handheld radio. "Lovell!"

"This is Lovell. We're moving to the back of the station," she said.

"We're at the front and ready to proceed."

From their vantage point, Spencer and his team could see the station. They were hidden behind a large van on Magnolia. Their next step would be to hit the station with tear gas, causing the men to run outside. He waited a few more long minutes, giving Lovell time to get into place on the back side of the station. His radio cracked to life.

"Ready when you are, Sergeant!" said Lovell from her concealed location at the back of the station.

"Gleason and Nix, you guys ready to hit them with the gas?"

Before they could answer, the street teemed with New Order men. Two cars drove toward the station and numerous New Order men seemed to spill from the neighboring buildings. This must have been where most of them lived, thought Spencer.

"Fire! We need to get them before they go inside!" he shouted.

Bullets flew from the police's weapons, cutting through the New Order men as they ran toward the safety of the station. Finally, several New Order men figured out the source of the gunfire and signaled the others to return fire. A wall of bullets hit the cops, who at first had the upper hand, and now were hopelessly pinned behind the van.

"We need to keep moving!" shouted Spencer.

"We can't, Sergeant! They have us nailed down!"

Spencer searched the area for an opportunity. They needed to get out from behind the van before the New Order men got even bolder.

Suddenly, numerous second-story windows of the pleasant-looking houses opened almost at once. Spencer could see the muzzles of rifles pointing at the New Order. Flashes of fire and the loud reports of gunfire erupted as citizens opened fire on the New Order, providing the cops with the opportunity to move from behind the van.

"Go now! Move!" shouted Spencer.

While under the protective fire, the officers moved to a location closer to the station, ready to hit the New Order with tear gas.

"We got this, Sergeant!" shouted Gleason as she and Nix sprinted toward the station with tear gas grenades in their hands.

They lobbed the cylindrical canisters through the windows of the station and sprinted for cover behind the nearest porch. Several seconds later, yellowish smoke started to pour from the open windows.

Men streamed out of the building, firing blindly as they went. Spencer and his officers cut the men down as they walked out of the front of the building.

Although he couldn't see the back side of the building, he could hear the thunderous sounds of live fire. He knew Lovell's team must have made it to the back of the station and were getting the New Order men as they tried to escape the building.

Chapter Fifty

The Boss had gotten up unusually early. He knew something was going to happen this morning. At first he thought he was just being paranoid, but within minutes of smoking his first cigarette, gunfire erupted from multiple directions throughout town, confirming his suspicions that the cops were back.

Darting from office to office, he looked out from the station at the chaos unfolding on the streets. As he watched his men being gunned down on the street by the cops and regular citizens shooting from their windows, he knew the second part of his plan needed to be executed. It was only a matter of time before they hit the station, killing everyone.

Turning to the men inside, he shouted, "Linc and Bet, get over here!"

"Shit, Boss. You see that? The cops are back! What do we do?" shouted a scared Linc.

"We get the fuck outta here! Put on these vests and helmets," he said, handing the men tactical gear. "It's quiet on the back side. We need to move back there and leave, fast!"

Other New Order men came into the tactical prep room.

"Everyone! Put this shit on. We're getting out of here!"

The men quickly started awkwardly dressing in the police tactical gear. The Boss knew the vests and helmets were of no use in a close-range gunfight, but he could care less about the idiots in the station.

All he needed to do was make it out the back and to his black SUV. Everything he needed to start his life again in a new location was in that SUV.

Grabbing the only three ballistic tactical shields in the prep room, he shouted to Linc and Bet.

"Here! Take these and listen. The three of us are moving out the back. You two first and then I'll follow," he said.

"No way, Boss. You see what's happening out there? No way," said Linc.

"This is the good shit. See these shields? Bullets can't get through them. They're for the SWAT teams. Now we need to get outta here before they hit us with more gas!"

He pushed the two scared men toward the back of the station. Neither seemed convinced that the shields would protect them, a sentiment the Boss shared, but he had no intention of dying inside a police station of all places.

"Move! Faster!" he yelled, nudging them from the back.

Men ran around the station, trying to get a good window in the front of the station to shoot from. Most of the men were shooting out of the front windows at the cops on the street, while others seemed almost paralyzed with fear and unsure of what to do.

"Alright, Bet, push the door open and get us out of here!"

Bet hesitated near the door. The Boss could tell the man would not go outside without a little encouragement. Looking outside to the parking lot, the Boss saw his black SUV and a random assortment of other vehicles. No cops were visible, but he knew better. Those sneaky assholes were good at hiding and waiting. He needed a distraction.

"Hey! The back is clear! The back is clear! Let's go!" he shouted into the station.

Frightened men heard his shouts and started streaming out the back doors. More tear gas canisters were lobbed through the open windows on the side of the building, filling the space with acrid smoke.

Turning to Linc and Bet, he shouted, "Now!"

Creating a shield with the bodies of Linc and Bet, the Boss slowly moved his way out of the building.

~ ~ ~

Kara Lovell and her team waited in concealed locations behind the police station. Too distracted by the shooting at the front of the station, none of the men had attempted to flee yet. Once the gas started pouring out of the windows, Lovell knew it would only be a matter of minutes before the men inside ran out, right into her squad's bullets.

She watched as two officers appeared near the side of the building and lobbed tear gas grenades inside. Soon the entire building would be filled with smoke. Within a few minutes, men started to scramble out of the toxic building, coughing and rubbing their eyes while firing blindly. Her team took them down without suffering any casualties.

Immediately after the first wave of men poured out of the building, a group of three emerged from the darkness. They wore tactical gear and carried ballistic shields, which she knew would be all but impenetrable to their rifles. Barely visible through the shields, she spotted a tall muscular man wearing a gas mask. The three moved in unison toward the parking lot. Bullets sparked off their shields, unable to reach the men behind them. Lovell knew they needed to do something fast or the men would get away. Before the squad could reposition, the tall man threw a grenade toward them, and her squad ducked. The grenade detonated with a flash and a deafening noise. She looked up in time to see another canister sail in their direction, forcing her to take cover again. The second grenade exploded in a billow of thick white smoke, partially obscuring her view of the tight phalanx of shields moving deeper into the parking lot.

Through the confusion, one man bolted out of the smoke toward a large black SUV with heavily tinted black windows, the engine roaring to life moments later. The two men he left behind threw down their bulky shields and ran after the SUV, but they fell victim to her squad's rifle fire before reaching their destination. Lovell concentrated her fire on the SUV, but failed to stop it. Bullets thumped into its sides and rear bumper as its squealing tires carried it out of the parking lot.

Other New Order cars screeched through town, heading in the same direction. Lovell heard the sound of bullets hitting the vehicles and assumed the veterans were shooting at the retreating men.

Bodies littered the back parking lot. The station's windows continued to billow acrid smoke. Slowly, the sound of nearby gunfire started to slow and then cease altogether.

Lovell's hands trembled as she gripped the handle of her weapon. She tried to focus her mind on her team's next move. The stress of battle left her momentarily stunned. She took several deep breaths to calm herself.

Chapter Fifty-One

Gayle and her team of veterans spread out along the main road leading out of Porter, spaced evenly behind trees and bumps of earth along the ground near the shoulder. She worried about Charlie. From the sound of the gunfight in town, the battle had been ferocious—but quick. It would just be a matter of time before her team would be needed.

"Charlie! What's the status up there? Over."

"The nests are clear, and the fighting has centered on the station. Over."

"Roger that! We're ready if they make a run for it."

Turning to the men and women near her, she yelled, "They're fighting at the station! We may get busy soon!"

The message was passed down the line. Surveying the people around her, she knew the veterans would do whatever it took to win this fight.

Less than a minute after Charlie's transmission, a large black SUV careened around the distant corner, heading straight toward them at an alarming rate of speed. A small sedan and a minivan followed the SUV closely. When the SUV straightened after the turn, it slowed and let the other vehicles pass. Gayle gave the order to fire when all three vehicles lined up to run their gauntlet.

The veterans started shooting immediately, striking the first vehicle with a maelstrom of lead. The windshield disintegrated from dozens of bullets, the sedan careening to the right and slamming into a ditch. Bullets pelted the minivan that followed, shattering most of its windows instantly. The occupants returned fire, skipping bullets off the ground and over the veterans' heads, but the heroes continued working their weapons, oblivious to the threat.

Without warning, the minivan swerved left and came to a sudden stop in the rough field. The exposed sliding door opened, disgorging a man with a shotgun, but he was dropped to the dusty ground before firing a shot.

The massive black SUV followed the minivan, but didn't have any trouble pushing through the field. It raced past the disabled vehicle, leaving a thick trail of dust in its wake. The veterans, encouraged by the defeat of most of the convoy, leapt out of their positions and advanced, firing bullet after bullet into the stopped vehicles.

"Get back to your positions! There may be more vehicles inbound!" Gayle shouted to the vets that ran after the retreating sedan.

The men and women quickly jogged back to their concealed places behind the trees or in the ditch.

"Gayle! What's your status!" shouted Charlie over Gayle's radio.

"Three cars headed in our direction. We were able to stop two of them but the SUV made it past us. Over."

"Injuries?"

"None."

The fog of adrenaline started to wear off, leaving Gayle nauseous and exhausted.

"We're going house to house, sweeping. Maintain your position until updated."

"Roger that. Over and out."

Chapter Fifty-Two

Grant stood motionless in the warehouse, watching for New Order men through the window. Since Mark and the other veteran had left him alone in the building, he'd alternated between the front and back windows. The back of the building gave him a view of the surrounding neighborhoods. Mark told him to watch the streets and take out any New Order men he saw. So far, he was able to stop several of them as they raced down the street, heading to the police station.

At first he worried he would have trouble identifying them. However, the New Order men were the only ones outside, except the cops. Besides, most of the men had a hard unmistakable meanness to them. Looking through the scope of his rifle, he focused in on movement from inside one of the houses. He could see the curtains being opened and closed like someone was trying to carefully peek outside. He'd keep careful watch on the house. Apparently, the New Order had moved into a lot of the houses downtown. He might've stumbled on one of their hideouts.

Carefully sighting the neat brick patio, he waited for the inhabitants of the house to make their move.

~ ~ ~

Marta and Brown spent the night in the basement. Brown insisted they go down there at night and not come out until the shooting ended. Marta thought it was a little bit of overkill but was happy to have someone thinking about her safety. After years of having no one to watch over her, Brown's attentions made her feel safe.

They set up sleeping bags in the dark, cramped basement. The sound of distant gunshots woke them just as the sun started to peek above the horizon. They only had two small basement windows to peer outside. The windows provided them with nearly no visibility to the streets. As the fighting intensified, she was happy to have only those small windows as the single vulnerable spots to their location.

Once the sound of fighting started to slow down and eventually stop altogether, they became restless.

"I'm going to check out what's happening," said Brown.

"No! You can't! It's not safe up there. We need to stay put. You said it yourself."

"There haven't been any gunshots for at least thirty minutes. Sounds to me like everything has ended."

"But who won? You can't go out there. If the cops are in control, they'll kill you."

"And if the New Order is in control, they'll do worse to you before they kill you," he said, pleading to her.

Marta knew Brown was right. She needed to stay safe until the police gave her the all clear to leave her house. Otherwise, she could walk into an angry mob of New Order men.

"Come on. You can come upstairs and look outside with me. If the coast is clear, I'll just go out the back door and have a look up and down the streets. I'll be gone for just five minutes."

She knew his plan made sense but still did not want to chance the safety of her new friend. Finally, out of curiosity more than anything, she relented.

"Okay, but just five minutes. Take a quick look, that's all."

"Yes, ma'am!" said Brown with a quick salute.

The two ascended the creaky basement stairs and emerged into the sunny kitchen. Marta pulled back the curtains from one of the back windows and carefully peered out. Brown stood at the door, looking out.

"You see? Nothing is happening. I'll just be a minute."

He opened the door and slipped outside onto her brick patio. She watched him move from the patio to the side of the house.

Suddenly, she heard the loud sound of rifle shots. Glancing at Brown, she saw him spin around in a strange dance. *What is he doing?* Then she realized he had been shot.

Without thinking, she opened the door and ran outside, screaming, "No! Stop shooting! Stop shooting!"

The rifle went silent, replaced by Marta's loud sobbing.

"Are you okay? Brown!"

He looked up at her and smiled slightly. "Could be better."

"Just hold on. I'll take care of you. Just hold on."

Looking at Brown's chest and shoulders, Marta knew there was nothing she could do for him. His injuries would require immediate medical intervention. Something she could not offer.

"Just hang in there, buddy," she said, cradling him.

His breathing became raspy as blood filled his lungs. Tears flowed freely from Marta's eyes, hitting Brown's face.

"Thank you. Thank you," she said over and over again.

He opened his eyes and said with a shaky, raspy voice, "For what?"

"Being my friend."

Chapter Fifty-Three

Sam tried to keep his mind off the day's events by busying himself in Doris's garden. Before leaving HQ, Doris had given Sam very strict instructions on what needed to be picked, pruned, watered and dug up. So far, he had been able to keep the garden in workable order. Although he guessed Doris wouldn't see it that way. Surveying the large garden, once again Sam was impressed by how easy Doris made it all seem. The garden was immense, more than a handful for even the most experienced gardener.

Standing by the well, Sam splashed large cups of water into his mug. The cool water was a welcome relief on such a hot day. Glancing at his watch again, he began to wonder if Jane would be one of the people sent to the house from HQ. If they were on bikes, they should have been to Doris's house already. He decided to check on Pritty in the comms shed to see if he'd heard anything.

The team decided to turn the radio on for fifteen minutes on the hour, every hour until the end of the thrust into Porter. Glancing at his watch yet again, it was five minutes until the top of the hour. Pritty would be turning on the radio and waiting for a signal from Porter. The few men and women left behind to guard Doris's house were nervous about this morning's operation. No one liked the odds. The police and veterans were outnumbered by the New Order men.

A damp, musty smell hit Sam as he opened the old wooden door to the shed. Closing the door behind him, he paused to give his eyes a moment to adjust to the gloomy interior. The sound of the generator outside became louder as he moved toward the portion of the shed occupied by the radio rig.

"Hey, Pritty. Hear anything yet?"

"Nothing for the last two check-ins. I'm worried about them. It's been hours since they should've moved into Porter. What do you think is happening?"

"I don't know. You're definitely right. I thought we would've heard something by now."

"They need to make it to Marta's house to contact us. Maybe that's the problem? Their handhelds won't be powerful enough given the distance."

"Good point. Have you been keeping the radio on until fifteen past the hour?"

"Yes, but I might extend that for the next two check-in points. An extra five minutes or so shouldn't affect the gas supply too terribly."

Suddenly, Pritty's handheld crackled to life. The officers guarding Doris's house used the handhelds to communicate with each other from their assigned lookout posts.

"Look alive, everyone, we have movement on the north trail," said one of the officers.

"I can see them coming but can't identify them yet. Hold one."

Sam and Pritty tensed, unsure of what to do. The comms shed was not exactly the best location to be in the case of an attack. Sam would have preferred to be in the house or hiding in the woods. A few tense seconds passed as the two waited for clarification.

"I have positive ID. It's Archer and Rapp. Repeat, it's Archer and Rapp! Stand down!"

Sam turned and ran from the shed, excited to see Jane.

She and Officer Rapp were riding bikes through the field to the house. She looked beautiful.

"Jane!" he shouted, waving.

Jane pulled her bike up next to Sam, kissing him quickly but not letting him hug her fully.

"I'm gross. I've been riding all morning. We would've been here sooner, but I popped a tire. The trail is brutal on these tires."

Sam didn't care about how gross she thought she was, he pulled her into his arms and held her, closing his eyes.

"I'm so happy to see you."

Finally breaking their embrace, he said, "Let's get you guys some water and lunch. You must be starving."

"Thirsty more than anything. We took some water this morning, but you know how it is at HQ. Boiling the water for drinking is such a hassle that we didn't want to take all of their purified reserves," said Rapp.

"Have you heard anything from Spencer or Charlie? How are things going?" said Jane as she leaned her bike against the side of the house.

"Nothing yet. We're supposed to check in on the hour. Hopefully, with the next call in, we'll get good news."

The three walked around the back of Doris's house to the well. Sam watched as Jane and Rapp each took deep gulps of cool water.

"What've you been doing? Your hands are mud crusted," asked Jane.

"Gardening. Doris asked me to keep things going for her. I'm doing the best I can, but really, it's a job for three people."

"I'm going to check in with everyone. See ya, Sam," said Rapp as he jogged toward the south entrance of the horse trail.

Sam and Jane moved to the rustic log seats around the unlit campfire. Sam gave her a couple of peppers and a handful of cherry tomatoes to snack on.

"How is Lea?"

"Worried. She didn't want me to leave, understandably. Neither did I, but I had no choice. An order is an order. I needed to come down here to help."

"I wondered if you would be one of the officers the chief sent. I hate having our family split up like this again. Once we get the all clear from town, we need to get back to HQ. I don't like leaving Lea alone."

"Me neither."

Kissing Sam quickly, Jane got up from her seat. "I need to go and check in with everyone. We'll catch up later."

Watching Jane walking toward the communications shed, Sam once again thought about how fortunate he was to have her.

Chapter Fifty-Four

Sitting on a picnic table, Lea watched as the kids sat eating their lunch. The food supply at the camp was dwindling. The fresh produce was long gone. Followed by the flour they used to make rustic tortillas. Then went all the dried milk, coffee, tea and powdered fruit drinks. The camp had a small garden, which produced some tomatoes, cucumbers and peppers, but nothing substantial. Lea figured that the kids must be hungry to eat white beans and canned tomatoes for three meals in a row.

"Can I have a popsicle?"

"We don't have popsicles," she replied with as little annoyance as she could muster. "Remember, silly, there's no power for the freezer."

The boy seemed satisfied with her answer. But she knew it was only a matter of time before a different child asked an equally out-of-touch question.

"Finish all the food you were given. Dinner is a long time away."

Lea wondered where Tank and his men were. Did he stay in Evansville or move on to another city? While shackled in the basement, she'd overheard the men talking about their supplies dwindling. They were mostly complaining about the cigarettes and booze. However, Lea knew it was only a matter of time before all the food would be gone.

She focused on Tank, wondering if he thought of her. Wondering if he was looking for her. Fear gripped her as a mental picture formed in her mind of returning to Tank's control. He was like a parasite that she just could not seem to shake off. Every time she pulled away, he pulled her back even harder. She felt reasonably safe at the camp. He had no way of knowing they were hiding there. Plus, with the guards posted around the perimeter, someone would see him before he made it anywhere near the camp. She hoped it was enough.

"Are you kids enjoying your succotash?" said Doris as she came out of the kitchen.

"Is that what you call this stuff?" said Lea.

"It is today," said Doris with a smile. "When we can get out of here and back to my house, I'll make you some real succotash with cornbread, right off my campfire," she said.

"Popsicles too?" said a little girl.

"Well, now that would be good!" said Doris. "I asked your daddy to tend to my garden until I can get down there. I'm hoping the squash is still alive."

"I don't think my dad knows anything about gardening," said Lea, laughing.

"Hey, Doris! Got any lunch left over? I'm starving," said Joyce.

"Sure! Give me just a minute," said Doris as she got up and went to the pot hanging over the campfire.

"How's it going with you, Lea?" asked Joyce.

"I'm pretty bored. Thinking about taking the kids to the lake after lunch for a swim."

"That sounds nice. It was pretty boring on watch too. Nothing to report except one car on the road. The driver went slowly past our entrance a number of times, like he was looking for something."

"What did you do?"

"Nothing. The chief said not to let anyone in unless they definitely looked like citizens. You know, parents of the kids or people on the move seeking shelter."

"What did the car look like? Could you see the driver?"

"It was a red Trans Am, with a black strip down the middle. I could only see that the driver was a large bald man. He didn't seem to be the kind to have a kid at the camp. So I stayed low. Eventually, he drove in. I told the chief, and in response, he doubled the guards on the front perimeter."

Lea shifted uncomfortably in her seat. A loud piercing sound buzzed in her ears as black splotches appeared in her field of vision.

"Lea! Are you okay? Put your head between your legs and breathe!"

Joyce shoved Lea's head down between her legs. Slowly, the sound abated and her vision returned to normal. Lea's heart continued to pound in her chest as she thought about Tank driving past the camp. Could it be him? Maybe it was someone with a similar car?

"There, that's better. You looked like you were passing out. I've never seen anyone go so white that fast," said Joyce.

"I'm okay. I just needed a minute. It's scary to think about the New Order men coming near here." Lea wiped the beads of sweat from her brow and tried to continue breathing deeply.

"I know. But don't worry. They can't get through the fence. Besides, we'll see them long before they could even try the fence. We're safe in here, honey. Sorry I scared you," said Joyce, patting Lea's shoulder.

Lea's mind twirled around horrific images of Tank. She knew Tank's rage would turn him into a monster. When he was like that, the only thing that seemed to calm him was beating her. The first punches were always the hardest. As his fists rained down on her, the force of them always started to subside, until they finally stopped. She knew Tank would be furious at her for escaping. His fury would also likely spill over to her parents, putting them and anyone else in his path in grave danger.

She fantasized about killing Tank over and over again. Perhaps this time she needed to act before he could hurt her or anyone else. Determination replaced fear in her mind as Lea formulated a plan.

Chapter Fifty-Five

After the surviving New Order vehicles raced out of town, the fighting died down considerably. Charlie knew the fight was over and they had won. Now they needed to be sure there weren't pockets of New Order men hiding amongst the civilians.

Dale Spencer jogged over to Charlie and his team as they reassembled on the street in front of the police station. The group stood upwind of the still-billowing acrid smoke that poured out of the station.

"Nice work, Charlie. I think the team of veterans really pushed us over the edge. And by the way, thanks for getting us out of the jam we were in. The New Order really had us pinned," said Spencer.

"Pinned? Wasn't us. All the veterans were busy taking out sniper nests. That's the information Marta had for us. The New Order had men placed all over town in concealed locations. We focused on clearing those spots so you guys could get in," said Charlie.

"Then where did the return fire come from?" said Spencer, glancing up at the houses on Magnolia. "There were people in all these houses, returning fire on the New Order."

One of the front doors opened and an upright-looking, awkward man peeked out. "Is it safe to come out?" he shouted.

Charlie and Spencer jogged over to the man.

"Not yet. We need to go through each building to be sure there aren't any New Order men still hiding in town. I'm Charlie, by the way, Evansville PD," said Charlie.

"I'm Dale Spencer, Porter PD. Were you with the guys returning fire on the New Order?" Spencer asked.

The man nodded, unsure what to say.

"Thanks for helping us! You guys saved our asses back there. Nice shooting," said Spencer, shaking the man's hand.

"Thanks. There're eleven houses down Magnolia as part of our team. We were waiting for you guys to bring the fight to the New Order before we jumped in. With only eleven of us, we didn't think we'd have much of a chance alone," said Henry.

"We weren't sure we had much of a chance either, but with your help, we did it!" said Spencer, giving the man's hand one last pump.

"Tell the other civilians to stay put for now until we give the all clear. I'm gonna take off. I need to radio HQ with an update," said Charlie.

Charlie left Spencer to form teams to go door-to-door. Right now he needed to make sure HQ and the team at Doris's house knew they'd reclaimed Porter. He also wanted them to know that one car got away. Gayle's team had been unable to stop the SUV as it careened across the field, out of range.

Turning the corner, Charlie headed to Marta's house. He hoped Marta and Brown had taken his advice and stayed put during the fighting. Bullets had a strange way of traveling; the last thing he wanted was Marta getting hurt.

Knocking on the front door of Marta's house, he waited for her to open up. He knocked again but heard no movement from inside. He decided to go to the back door. If she was still in the basement, she might hear a knock at the patio door better than the front door. He rounded her house and nearly stumbled on Brown's outstretched legs.

"Holy shit! Marta, what happened?"

"He went out to check to see if it was safe and someone shot him!" she yelled through sobs.

Charlie could tell that Brown was dead. He figured Marta must have been sitting with him in that condition for a little while.

Grabbing her arm, he said, "Come on, let's get you inside."

She slowly let go of Brown and allowed Charlie to move her back inside her house. Once Marta was seated on her couch, Charlie disappeared into the kitchen and whispered into his handheld for Mark.

"Mark, you copy?"

"It's Mark. We're going through the houses on Smith Road. All clear so far."

Charlie knew Smith Road was not too far from Marta's location. Mark could easily direct a couple of members of his squad to pull Brown's body from Marta's backyard.

"Brown is dead. He was shot coming out of Marta's house. Can you have someone come by to grab him? Marta is really upset."

"Crap, sorry, man. We'll be right over. Out."

Charlie joined Marta on the couch again.

"I'm sorry about Brown. I know he had become a friend. And he was an invaluable asset to the police, a real hero. Without him, our officers would've been gunned down by the New Order snipers; things could have turned out very differently. Everyone was right where he said they'd be."

Charlie could tell his words made Marta feel a little better. She looked up and smiled slightly.

"Can I use the radio? I need to contact HQ. The police station is still toxic from the tear gas we used to flush them out."

"Is it over?" she asked, a little stunned.

"Mostly, we just need to go through the houses and businesses to be sure there aren't any men hiding."

Marta's shoulders dropped and she exhaled. "I can't believe it's really over. I can actually go outside!" She got up and headed toward the front door.

"Not yet. We'll give the all clear. For now, let's call HQ."

"Right, sorry. I've lived like a shut-in for so long the thought of getting into the sunshine was overwhelming. Come on, let's make that call!"

The two walked quickly up the stairs into the attic. Marta uncovered the radio and turned it on.

"It's all yours!"

Glancing at his watch, Charlie realized they had a few minutes before the designated communications time.

"I need to wait until the top of the hour. We agreed to communicate only at that time in order to save power."

The two sat in companionable silence, waiting for time to pass. Finally, Charlie picked up the handheld and said, "Blue Jay, this is Overlook One. Come in. Blue Jay, this is Overlook One. Over."

"This is Blue Jay. Hearing you loud and clear, Overlook One. What's your status?"

"The Town of Porter is secure. Repeat, the Town of Porter is secure! We're just doing the final cleanup."

"Congratulations! And excellent work!"

"Thank you! We did have one black SUV escape our grip. We think it only contained one individual. Over."

"Roger that, we'll be on the lookout. Any blue casualties? Over."

"Two officers and one veteran are down, with multiple others injured. Over."

"Sorry to hear it. We'll alert HQ."

Charlie turned off the radio and looked at Marta. The two weary friends had been through so much.

"I can't believe it's really over," she said.

"From one perspective. At least the New Order is no longer in Porter." Standing up, Charlie stretched and then said, "I need to get back out there to help search. Please stay put until we give the all clear."

The two walked down the creaky steps. Marta opened the front door and inhaled deeply.

"I don't ever remember the air smelling so sweet."

Chapter Fifty-Six

Tank drove back into Evansville after spending the morning looking for Camp Hemlock. He was convinced that Lea and her family were hiding at the kids' camp. The problem was that he couldn't find the place. The camp was located in a rural area near Lake Sparrow. Only one main road led up into that entire region.

Looking at the map, he figured finding the place would be a cinch, but of course it wasn't. He wasted precious fuel driving back and forth looking for the camp. There was just nothing up there. Seemingly endless walls of thick forest lined the road, with only the occasional glimpse of the lake. There was no road sign for the camp or road sign indicating he had made it there. Finally, frustration got the better of him and he called it a day.

The closer he got to town, the more anxious he became. Explaining his failure to the guys would not be easy. They would sense weakness and perhaps even make inroads to threatening his control over them. Bower had told him not to go. He'd said it would be a waste of fuel. He knew Bower was wrong. It wasn't a waste of time or fuel. That bitch and her parents were up there. He could just feel it.

On his way back, he stopped at the one marina that serviced Lake Sparrow. The sleepy marina consisted of a store and small pier. Not exactly a maritime hub but adequate for the small boats of vacationers who used the lake. The glass door to the store shattered with a loud smashing sound under the weight of his boots. It was obvious that no one had been in the marina. The marina's store contained all the usual boating shit with the addition of a small candy aisle. He greedily grabbed candy bars, chips, gum, mints and anything else he could shove into bags, stuffing candy bars in his mouth two at a time. He would share a portion of the loot with the guys, proving his trip was worthwhile. Then he would stash the rest of it in case he and Bower needed to bolt.

Getting back into his Trans Am, he started to pull out of the marina's lot but then realized that he hadn't checked the couple of vehicles in the lot for fuel. Sure enough, the cars had plenty of gas. He filled up his tank, along with several gallon tanks, which he stored in his trunk. The fuel supply would not be shared with the group. If he and Bower needed to make a run from town, the fuel would come in handy. On the other hand, if he found Lea, he could bring her along instead of Bower. There were advantages to having her with him.

Tank drove to the center of Evansville, to the location of their new headquarters. The restaurant had never been good when it was open; at least it was worth something closed, thought Tank with a slight smirk. Turning the corner, he could see a large black SUV parked in front of his headquarters. *What the fuck?* He didn't recognize the truck. The SUV's sides and back were covered in bullet holes, its windows shattered. Whoever drove this truck came out of some serious shit, he thought.

Tank walked into the restaurant with his usual, take-charge air, curious to see who had washed up on his doorstep.

"Tank, my man! Nice of you to join us. The guys told me you've been out looking for your old lady. Said you can't keep the woman in one place!" said the Boss to a round of laughter.

The Boss sat in Tank's seat, surrounded by his men. The New Order men looked at Tank with renewed hatred. Their Boss was in charge now and Tank would have to listen to him or face the consequences. He could tell the men were anxious for a misstep, giving them an excuse to pummel him.

"Looking for some skinny-assed dumb bitch? Fuck that. I was out finding all of this!" said Tank, spilling the candy bag open on the table in front of the Boss.

The men quickly descended on the candy, grabbing anything they could get their dirty hands on. The Boss remained still, staring at Tank. Tank defiantly returned the stare, despite knowing stepping up was probably not good for his long-term survival. He couldn't help himself; he hated guys like the Boss. A two-bit gangbanger thinking he was a god because a few losers followed him.

"What the fuck happened to your truck?" he asked, breaking the stony showdown.

Finally the Boss broke his stare and responded, "The cops are back in Porter, and I'm the only one to survive their little shit storm."

The intense look on the Boss's face told Tank to shut up or get a bullet in the eye.

"Sorry, man, you had some decent guys on your crew," said Tank, taking a different approach.

He needed to figure out if the Boss intended to stay or if he was just passing through.

"But now I've got another crew, all ready for me, right here," said the Boss, jutting his chin forward in a challenge.

Tank knew his guys could not take on the Boss's gang. Looking around the room, he caught Bower's eye. Bower silently pleaded with him to yield. The last thing they needed was to get into a turf war over Evansville. He would stand down and then figure out a way to kill that asshole the Boss.

"Looks like you guys won't skip a beat in Evansville. You'll be comfortable here, that's for sure."

"We will. And speaking of comfortable, I decided to move into the large Victorian house next door. The guys said you wouldn't mind relocating," said the Boss to not so quiet laughter. "Bower has all of your shit. I suggest you find another spot to rest your head."

That motherfucker. Tank could barely control his fury. He could feel his jaws lock into place as his fists curled tight. Staring at the Boss, Tank thought about ramming his fist into the man's head and then smashing his head against the floor until it popped open like a pumpkin.

"Hey, man! Let's go! I'll show you where we're staying," said Bower, with a strong hand on Tank's arm.

Tank knew Bower had saved him from more than one bad move over the years.

Bower leaned into Tank and whispered, "Let's go before you get us killed."

The Boss sat staring at Tank with that smug, condescending look. Not taking his eyes off the Boss, Tank vowed to be with the man when he took his last breath.

Bower shoved Tank out of the restaurant and onto the street. Tank could barely think through the haze of adrenaline.

"Fuck! What were you doing in there? Trying to get us killed? You need to chill the fuck out!"

"You see the way he looked at me? Like some chump. This is *my* town!"

"Yeah, well, we don't have the guys to take on his gang. And they would love nothing more than to shave us. You need to play it cool. Those guys won't last. Look at his truck! The cops are back and there's only one group they'll be looking for, those New Order gangbangers. You and me, we're just innocent civilians."

Tank visibly calmed. He'd never thought of it that way, but Bower was right. The cops would be looking for the prisoners that escaped, not innocent civilians. They needed to distance themselves from the Boss and the others or get killed with them.

"Did you catch what he said? He's the only one that survived Porter?" asked Tank.

"I know. I thought they had, like, forty guys. Fuck that. I'm not dying with those shits. When the cops come back, we go back to being regular citizens. Those shits either get killed or go back to prison. Maybe we need to leave town while we can?" asked Bower as they walked toward their new home.

"No way. They'll be watching for us to make a move. We need to lie low. I grabbed more candy, gas and some clothes from a marina on Lake Sparrow. I only brought in a little of the stash for those goons. We need to keep our supply hidden and ready to move out. As soon as I find Lea, we make a break for it."

"Lea? Are you shitting me? We need to go before the cops get here and kill all of us!" said Bower, raising his voice.

Tank slammed his friend up against the side of the building and grabbed his shirt. "I said we go after I get Lea back! I'm not leaving here without that bitch! You got it!"

Giving Bower one more hard shove, Tank walked away.

Chapter Fifty-Seven

Mark and Marty Stevens, one of the veterans, walked into the last restaurant on the main road in Porter. It was a diner-style place with a fifties motif that had probably served really good fries and burgers. Mark opened the door and signaled for Stevens to go to the right while he went to the left. The two men fanned out and started their quick search. They had been through the entire town, finding nothing. The search felt more like an obligation than a potentially dangerous mission.

The entire seating area could be seen from the front door. The men easily confirmed that no one was hiding in the room. Mark went to check the bathrooms while Stevens went into the kitchen. He went into the ladies' room first, checking each stall carefully, finding nothing. Then he checked the men's room, again finding nothing. Glancing in the mirror, he took a chance that there could still be water in the line and tried the faucet. Sure enough a little water followed by a huge burst of air came out. Mark cupped his hands and rinsed his sweaty, grimy face, exhaling at the simple pleasure of being clean.

The loud crack of gunfire erupted in the restaurant outside the men's room. Unsure of who was shooting or if Stevens was okay, Mark needed to act fast. He quietly moved to the door and inched it open, peering into the restaurant. From his vantage point, he could see two New Order men standing in the restaurant, looking out onto

Main Street. Stevens was nowhere in sight. They must have shot him. *Damn it. I'm in here washing while he's getting shot.*

Anger welled in Mark. He'd become so complacent about the mission that he'd left one of his men open to an attack, costing the man his life. There was no way he could let the New Order escape the restaurant and potentially hurt more people in town. Suddenly his radio cracked to life, exposing his position. Both New Order men turned and looked in the direction of the men's bathroom. Mark knew they would not be able to see him well, if at all, without the aid of flashlights. They were standing in a sunny part of the restaurant and he was in a pitch-black shadowy corner.

The men reacted quickly, turning and shooting into the darkness. Mark dove to the ground and returned fire, hitting the first man and killing him instantly. Blood from the first man sprayed onto the face of the stunned second man, who continued to shoot and sought the safety of the long serving counter for cover. The man leaped over the counter and fell silent. Mark sat on the floor just outside the men's room, partially hidden by the door frame leading to the restrooms.

"Stevens!" yelled Mark, although he knew the man was likely dead. "Stevens! You still with me?"

"Charlie, this is Mark. We have an active shooter in the Rocking Fifties restaurant. Stevens is down. Repeat. Active shooter in the Rocking Fifties."

"What is your location?" asked Charlie.

"I'm inside the restaurant with him."

A long pause followed. Mark knew Charlie was trying to process a way in which to help him.

"You know you aren't getting out of here," said Mark to the New Order man.

"Fuck you! I ain't going back to that shithole PrisCorp prison!"

The New Order man made a run for the back kitchen, giving Mark the opening he was waiting for. Mark blasted a concentrated ring of bullets in the man's direction, hitting him in multiple locations on his chest and head. The man slumped to the ground, leaving a long red stain on the kitchen door.

Nudging the man's lifeless leg with the edge of his boot, Mark said, "No one said anything about sending you back to PrisCorp."

Running to the back room, Mark went to check on Stevens.

"Shooter has been neutralized. Repeat. Shooter down."

Stevens lay in a pool of blood on the floor of the kitchen. A faint pulse pumped in his neck. Ripping the man's shirt open, Mark inspected him for gunshot wounds, finding a gaping hole in his upper right shoulder. Unconscious and likely in shock, the man needed medical attention immediately.

"Mark!" yelled Charlie from inside the restaurant.

"In here!"

Charlie burst into the kitchen, waving his flashlight around to find Mark and Stevens in the back.

"How bad is he?" asked Charlie.

"I don't know, but it looks like a clean shot. He needs medical attention."

"Alright, let's get him to the church. The father there opened the doors and announced he has food, water and medical supplies. He's taking in our injured."

"No shit?"

"Yeah, apparently the New Order didn't hit the church. The father has been sneaking food around town since the whole thing started. He's an amazingly brave man."

Walking out into the sunshine, Mark and Charlie carried Stevens to the church a couple of blocks away. People were coming out of their homes, congregating in the streets, hugging each other and crying. Mark assumed they were crying with relief that their ordeal was finally coming to a close.

"Father! We've got another one for you!" shouted Charlie as they moved through the front doors of the church.

"Put him over here! I've got a cot ready!" shouted Father Roy.

Father Roy had pulled out cots, blankets and jugs of water for the injured. He'd even set up a table of medical supplies to assist the nurse and doctor who were treating the wounded. Four men lay on the cots.

"Thanks, Father. It's amazing that you have all these supplies. The New Order left you alone?" said Mark in shock.

"I'm not surprised. It's the power of God, my friend. None of them want to mess with the big guy," said Father Roy, chuckling.

"I guess not! Why does the church have so many supplies?" said Mark.

"Part of our mission is to support the homeless. In the summer, the place is nearly empty, but in the winter, this entire area is filled with cots. We provide shelter, food and some basic first aid. Looks like we now have a different sort of community to care for."

"Mark, I need to get back to the station. The place is aired out enough for us to get in there. You want to join me?" asked Charlie.

"Sure."

"Nice meeting you, Father Roy, and thanks again," said Mark.

The two men left the church, making their way through the people who were slowly migrating toward the house of worship in search of assistance.

Chapter Fifty-Eight

Jane and Sam sat close together by the light of the campfire. The few officers at Doris's house rotated through a watch-standing schedule. Jane was not due to stand her second watch for another hour. She was relieved to have the time alone with Sam before they headed back to HQ.

Euphoria had spread once Pritty announced that Porter had been retaken by the police. Everyone was in a light, happy mood, hopeful about the future.

"When do you want to leave for HQ?" asked Sam, interrupting her thoughts.

"I think we need to leave before first light. I want to get back to Lea as soon as possible." Jane snaked her arm through Sam's and nuzzled closer to him.

"I agree. The longer we're away from her, the more likely something will happen. Everyone is in such an amazing mood. I don't want to spoil it. But really, we can't go home. The New Order is still an active threat in Evansville and maybe other places we don't know about."

"I know, but I think people just need a break to enjoy one success before moving to the next battle."

"The chief said he wants to move HQ down here; that'll keep people busy. The Evansville PD has loads of supplies up at HQ. It'll take a while to transport everything down here."

"I think a lot of the tactical supplies were used in the Porter battle. There may not be a lot left at this point. But moving here makes a lot of sense. Fresh well water and abundant food make this farm ideal."

"Do you think Doris will mind?" asked Sam, stroking her hair.

"Mind? Are you kidding? Doris loves being in the middle of things. You should've seen her at HQ. She was in her glory feeding everyone. I think Doris will be just fine."

"Speaking of being in the middle of things, how long do you have before your shift?" said Sam into her ear with a breathy voice.

"Less than thirty minutes."

"That should do," he said, smiling and pulling her up into his arms.

Jane and Sam walked arm and arm into the tent they shared.

Chapter Fifty-Nine

Lea lay on her cot in the cabin she had shared with her parents. Since both of them were gone, she found it increasingly hard to fall asleep. The night sounds frightened her. She kept thinking about Tank driving slowly past the camp's entrance, searching for her. It was only a matter of time before Tank figured out which road led into the camp. Removing the signs would only hide their location for so long. He'd figure it out. He always managed to find her.

Her stomach burned, an acidy nervousness as she thought about Tank searching for her. She needed to do something to stop him. Lying on the lumpy cot, she weighed her various options. Staying and waiting for him to find her was not possible. If he found this place, he would hurt or kill anyone in his way to get to her. Then he would steal their supplies and ruin or take the radios. No way would she allow that to happen to the nice people staying at the camp. Not to mention the kids. She would not let anything happen to the little gang of kids put in her charge. They might be annoying, but they were counting on her to keep them safe. Witnessing one of Tank's rampages would not be good for any of them.

No, she needed to take action. If she could just ruin his car, that would slow him down. Then all she needed to do was injure him enough to keep him from doing any more searching. She just needed to slow him down. Yes, that was it. She just needed to slow him down. That would give the cops time to move into Evansville and clear the mess up, including Tank. Just like they did in Porter. Slow him down. But how?

Gazing at the stars outside her window, she listened to the lone call of a barn owl. The owl's hooting took on a sinister tone as it mixed in her mind with thoughts of Tank. The forest seemed to close in on her, as every shadow appeared to be Tank hiding, looking for her.

Again, she thought about waiting for her mom and dad to come back, but quickly discounted the idea. They would tell her to stay at the camp and be safe. Let the police handle Tank, they would say. But she knew this was not an option. Her being at the camp created immeasurable danger to everyone there. They just didn't know it and wouldn't listen to her warnings. She needed to take care of the problem she'd caused by opening the door to him when the lights first went out.

Tossing and turning, she finally settled on a position on the cot that was slightly more comfortable than any of the others she had tried. Closing her eyes, she willed herself to sleep one last time.

Chapter Sixty

Sam put the rest of his meager personal effects into his backpack, preparing to leave. Jane had been up long before him and had previously packed. He knew she had been on watch most of the night, yet her energy persisted. She buzzed around the farm, getting coffee and checking in with everyone in preparation for their departure.

Charlie, Spencer and a couple other Evansville officers were en route to Doris's house. Eventually, most of the Porter and Evansville police departments would converge at the farm in preparation to take over Evansville. Getting Charlie and a few others back to the farm was just their first step. Jane figured they would show up around noon. She offered to stay until relieved, but the officers at Doris's house told her to get moving back to HQ. They would hold down the fort until the others came.

Sam knew she was more than excited to be getting back to Lea, as he was. Zipping up the small tent, he made sure it was completely secure for when they came back. The last thing he wanted was to show up to a tent full of water and bugs.

"Hey, sleepyhead, you about ready to get out of here?" yelled Jane across the lawn.

"Sure. I'll grab some fruit and more water for our walk before we roll out," he said, walking over to her.

She walked toward him, putting her arms around his waist,

hugging him. "You're getting too slim. We need to feed you more. Grab some of the walnuts in the kitchen Doris has so much of; you can stand to eat a little more," she said, kissing him gently.

"I guess you're right. I have been really trying not to eat in order to save some for others. But the few pairs of shorts I have are literally falling off my frame. I guess a few extra walnuts won't hurt the overall picture. I'll be right back."

Sam walked into the calm farmhouse kitchen. Memories of sitting at the table with Charlie and Doris flooded back to him. The last time he and Jane were here, they had just come back from the mountains and were trying like hell to get home to Lea. Now they were again leaving to get to Lea, only this time things were much better. Finding the walnut jar, Sam shook out half the Mason jar into a small container. Jane was right, he needed to eat a little more or he would not be able to help anyone.

"Okay, all set," he said to Jane as she waited for him.

Hand in hand, the two walked toward the trail.

"How do you think she has been doing since you left her?" asked Sam.

"She was really worried about me coming down here, but she's mostly fine. The kids are driving her crazy. Although, I think that was the best job the chief could've given her. The little collection of rug rats keeps her mind off things, even if she won't admit it."

"Well, if you ever hope to have grandkids, maybe we should request a reassignment for her. She was never into kids. This could push her over the edge," said Sam, chuckling.

Chapter Sixty-One

Charlie sat with Gayle at the church, finishing a light breakfast. The church seemed to have a near endless supply of food and drinking water in its pantry. Many of the officers, including Charlie and Gayle, had slept in the church the night before in between their watch rotations. The church's location made an excellent barracks for the veterans and officers, and the father seemed thrilled to assist the good men and women that had liberated the town.

Before nightfall, the police went through all the known places where the New Order stayed to retrieve weapons, food, medications and anything else useful that the New Order had stolen from the people of Porter. The supplies were brought to the station and held for distribution to Porter's citizens. Getting weapons in the hands of the citizens of Porter would be essential in assisting the officers to maintain the city from any renewed attacks by the New Order or any other such group.

Charlie looked at Gayle while he finished his breakfast, the glitter of her engagement ring moving as she ate. He felt profoundly lucky to have her by his side. Anything could have happened in yesterday's attack. They were fortunate to have survived uninjured.

"What are you thinking about?" asked Gayle, catching him staring at her.

"How lucky I am. You did an amazing job yesterday, holding the road."

"Not really, one SUV got away on us."

"But the other vehicle didn't and none of your people were hurt. That's the important thing."

"I guess. It just would have been nice to stop all three vehicles from leaving. You about finished up? You should get to the station and I need to relieve the trail watch."

"In a few more days, I think we should move back to your house. Mine won't be habitable for a while after what they did to it."

"The habitability of your place was always in question," she said with levity.

"Nice," said Charlie, grabbing her hand and lifting her to her feet.

Getting up from the church pew, Charlie stretched and yawned. The stress of the past weeks was starting to take a toll on his body. Physical exertion, lack of sleep, inadequate nutrition and near constant anxiety had a way of slowing a person down. Once they got the police station running, Charlie and Gayle would be able to take a slight breather and get some space from the others. As much as Charlie liked the other officers and veterans, he was starting to feel the need for some distance.

"Give me a kiss. I need to head this way to get to the trailhead," said Gayle, kissing him lightly.

"See you this afternoon at the station."

Charlie jogged the short distance to the station. Officers and veterans were coming and going as the watch changed shifts.

"Charlie! All the Porter PD weapons we retrieved from the town are in the armory," said Mark, approaching Charlie as he walked into the station.

"Did you do an assessment of the weapons and ammo to see how much the town has left?" asked Charlie.

"We did. I've compiled a list for you," said Mark, handing the list to Charlie. "I also have the inventory list from before everything happened as a comparison."

Glancing at the two lists, Charlie compared the police

department's weapons cache from before and after the New Order's attack.

"Seems like a sizable number of the department's tactical firearms are missing."

"How many?" said Mark.

"Several. A sniper rifle, six assault rifles, two shotguns and three MP5s," said Charlie.

"The good stuff," said Mark.

Charlie nodded.

"We have no reason to believe that any of the citizens stole the weapons. That only leaves one place where they went," said Mark.

"The SUV that got away."

"Exactly. Whomever was in that SUV had planned for a quick departure. Can't see any other explanation."

"I agree. We need to update HQ. They need to know what is floating around out there. For all we know, the guy who left with this stuff intends to reassemble a team and make another hit on Porter. Let the watch standers know," said Charlie.

"Got it," said Mark.

"Good morning!" said Bill Reynolds as he approached the station. "I don't know about you guys, but I never had such an amazing sleep. It feels good to have our town back."

"For now. We were just talking about the missing weapons from the station's arsenal. Seems like whoever left did so with a fairly large stash. I need you to assemble the veterans and any willing citizens for a citizen's militia. We'll start distributing the remaining weapons this afternoon. We need to look sharp and be ready for another attack," said Charlie.

"Sure thing. I know all the vets will be in and I'm sure the eleven guys who basically created a shooting arcade on Main Street would be willing to participate. In addition, we'll go door-to-door, asking for volunteers," said Reynolds.

"That'll be great. I want everyone to know that even though we had this one victory, we're far from being completely safe. Everyone in town needs to be ready to fight. We can distribute the weapons, arming all citizens who have weapons experience," said Charlie.

"I'll get right on it. I'm sure there are many citizens who would be willing to be part of a citizens' militia. I'll get one of the vets to head it and organize their team," said Reynolds.

"That should work. Mark, I need you to take control of the armory. You can handle the weapons distribution. Also, take any of the hoarded New Order food out of the station and give it to Father Roy. He can handle food distribution. He's already doing that and is very good at giving people just what they need," said Charlie.

"I'll have the weapons cleaned and ready for distribution this afternoon. The food we can move right away. I'll grab a couple of guys and start making that happen," said Mark.

Officers Cleff and Rogers walked past the three, heading out to the front lawn. Cleff slowly unfastened the flagpole's rope while Rogers handed him the flag. Together they hoisted the United States Flag and the City of Porter flag and the flag for the City of Porter's Police Department. Charlie was surprised by his emotional response to seeing the flags flying. He thought about the brave officers who were victims of the New Order and all those who fought to free the town. The fight was by no means finished, but they would make it, one step at a time.

Chapter Sixty-Two

Jane and Sam made better time getting back to HQ than Jane would have thought. She always considered Sam to be a slow walker and assumed that they would add an extra hour or two to their journey because of his pace. However, today, he seemed as anxious to get back to HQ and Lea as she did. After being admitted through a hole in the fence on the south side of the property, Jane could not stop thinking about seeing Lea and then jumping in the lake for a refreshing rinse.

The smooth, serene lake glistened in the afternoon sun, beckoning her to jump in. She knew the refreshing waters would do her aching feet and back wonders. Later, she would have to go to the camp's lost and found to see if she could grab an extra set of shoes. Her hiking boots were quickly deteriorating into two very painful blister-causing torture devices.

The main lodge sat in the distance. Its broad beam porches and three-story frame contrasted beautifully with the deep green forest. Jane thought the place looked more like a rich person's mountain hideaway than a kids' camp.

"Finally, almost there," said Sam.

"I thought we made pretty good time, considering."

"Considering what?"

"Well, you always seem to walk a little slowly, but not today. You were moving faster than I expected. I originally thought we'd be lucky to get here by dinner."

Laughing and mocking feigned insult, Sam said, "Are you saying I actually feel like a ball and chain, slowing you down?"

"No. More like an anchor."

Jane grabbed his hand, softly squeezing it and smiling.

"Where do you think Lea is?" she asked as they approached the lodge.

"Don't know. Let's go inside and see who's around."

Walking into the lodge, Jane was struck at how silent the place was. Most of the officers were either down in Porter or at Doris's house. The HQ contained only a fraction of the number of people that were there the first time they arrived at the camp. The place seemed deserted.

"Hello?" Jane shouted into the empty lodge.

Sunlight streamed into the lodge through the floor-to-ceiling western-facing windows in the lodge's main gathering room.

"Hello?" she yelled again.

"Where is everyone?" asked Sam.

"Beats me. You'd think the kids would be around."

"Anybody home?" yelled Sam toward the dining area.

"Back here!" came a reply.

The door to the kitchen swung open. Doris greeted them cheerily, wiping her hands on her apron. "Hey, guys! You just getting back?"

"Yeah, where is everybody?" asked Jane.

"There aren't many people left, just a few officers and families. I think most of the officers, including the chief, are standing watch. They all seem to rotate in and out of here at odd times."

"Have you seen Lea?" asked Sam.

"No, sorry. I haven't seen her all day."

"Okay, we'll see you later. We're going to go look for her," said Jane.

"Alright. If the two of you need a snack or anything, just come back. I'm making dinner but can get you something to tide you over, if needed."

"Thanks, Doris," said Sam over his shoulder.

Sam and Jane walked back outside toward the center of the camp. Only the sounds of the forest greeted their searching ears. They couldn't hear Lea or the kids she usually spent her day with.

"Let's go and check the cabin. Maybe she didn't feel well and is taking a nap?" said Sam.

Joyce Rolz walked steadily up the road in their direction. Jane assumed she must've been coming from her watch-standing rotation at the entrance to the camp.

"Hey, Joyce!" shouted Jane.

"Hey, guys, you just get back?" said Joyce, jogging toward them.

"We did and are looking for Lea. Have you seen her?" asked Sam.

"No, I haven't. I assumed the chief has her doing something other than babysitting because this morning I saw Patty Epstein with the kids."

Laughing slightly, Jane said, "Well, Lea really didn't like babysitting. Maybe she finally convinced the chief to move her. Anything else happening?"

"Not really. It's been very quiet here. No new families have arrived, but one car has been driving down the main road pretty consistently," said Joyce.

"One car? What do you mean? What sort of car?"

"A red Trans Am with one large bald man driving. He keeps driving the main road like he's looking for something. We haven't flagged him down because he doesn't look like a parent or lost citizen."

Jane could feel her legs buckling at Joyce's description of a person who could only be Tank.

"Oh crap. That sounds like our daughter's ex-boyfriend Tank. Did he have neck tattoos? Could you tell?" asked Sam.

"I'm not sure about the neck tattoos, but he seemed like a really big guy from how he was seated in the car. So far he hasn't stopped, but the chief has us doing extra watches to accommodate a larger presence at the road side of the camp."

"That's a good idea. If it is Tank, he is extremely dangerous and has been working with the New Order. He cannot be let into the camp under any circumstances," said Jane.

"If you see Lea, would you tell her we're back?" said Sam, taking Jane's hand and pulling her toward the trail to the cabin.

"See ya, Joyce. I'll check in with the chief later to help with the watch," said Jane.

The two walked quickly down the narrow trail leading to their cabin.

"Tank is in the area? That can't be good news. And he looks like he's looking for something? That's even worse," said Jane.

The screen door banged loudly against the wooden frame of the cabin. Their eyes quickly adjusted to the gloom inside the one-room, open structure. A single sheet of paper sat on Jane's cot. She grabbed it and read silently.

Looking up at Sam, she said, "She's gone. The note says she went to find Tank. Something about wanting to slow him down."

Handing the note to Sam, Jane sank to the cot, crestfallen. She stared at the floor as Sam read the note.

"Damn her. What the hell is she thinking?" he said.

"She's brave and stubborn. That's not always the best combination."

"We need to find her before she does anything stupid."

"You mean anything else stupid. Where do we start our search? She could be anywhere in town by now," said Jane, rubbing her brow.

"We should start at the storage locker. Maybe she decided to go there first? Or, I don't know, maybe home?"

"No, there's no way she went back to our house. She told me she would never want to sleep in that house again. I think you're right.

We start with the storage locker. Who knows, maybe if our stuff is still there, she'll decide to rest at the locker and we'll be able to find her."

"Alright. Let's get going, unless you need more time to rest before setting out again," asked Sam.

"I'm good. I just want to find her."

"Me too."

Jane couldn't believe they were heading out looking for Lea. Part of her wanted to strangle their daughter for being so reckless. Part of her admired Lea's strength and bravery. Jane knew Lea was doing what she thought was right.

Chapter Sixty-Three

The Boss sat at Tank's usual table in the restaurant, talking to the guys as they came and went. He didn't particularly like running things from the restaurant, but since that hulking man Tank returned to town, he needed to hold the position so Tank knew he had been dethroned. The Boss relished seeing Tank's expression when he realized he had been replaced. Nothing gave the Boss more pleasure than watching Tank try to decide how to respond. Fight, flight or fall in line. Of course Tank chose to fall in line. There were not many men alive who chose fight when confronted with the same set of circumstances.

Although Tank did a decent job of pretending to fall in line with the Boss's control of the town, the Boss just didn't trust the man. There was something going on that he could not put his finger on. The Boss suspected Tank of hiding supplies. But then again, he suspected everyone to be hoarding his own stash. Things were starting to get more desperate. It would be stupid not to be looking out for one's own interests. No, it was something more than that.

Turning to one of his men, the Boss said, "Hey, Paulie, next time that asshole Tank rolls out of here in his seventies-style shit can of a car, I want you guys to follow him. Not too close, though. I want to know where he's going."

"You got it, Boss. He usually disappears in the late afternoon. We'll spook him. Who knows what we'll find."

"He's up to something. I can just feel it."

"I'll get Rico and Jones on it. Rico is like a fucking basset hound, man. He can find anything. There's no way Tank'll know they're spooking him."

Satisfied, the Boss got up from the table and stretched. Looking out the window, the Boss contemplated leaving the stifling restaurant but then thought better of it.

"Any more new arrivals?" he asked Paulie.

"Just the guys from Grant that came yesterday. I suspect we'll see more and more of them streaming in."

Numerous PrisCorp prisoners were on the move in the general area. Some had initially stayed in and around Grant, the location of the prison. As time went by, those men started moving in a steady stream westward, into Evansville. The Boss was able to recruit most of them into his army by flashing the cache of weapons he had stolen from Porter's and Evansville's Police Departments. However, he had to deflect uncomfortable questions from the guys about what happened in Porter. He knew the men would be nervous about the cops pulling off another coup, even if some of them were too afraid of him to mention it. He needed a surefire safe place to rebuild his empire; maybe he'd found it in Evansville, maybe not. Only time would tell.

For now, the Boss was determined to rebuild his army with the men who came from Grant. Only this time, he would make it stronger and larger than before. He would not let the cops retake Evansville or any other place he called home. Nor would he let that two-bit thug Tank interfere with his goals.

Chapter Sixty-Four

Lea moved steadily through the woods, roughly following a narrow trail toward Evansville. The trail ran parallel to the road to Evansville. She knew Tank would have driven that road in order to get to the camp. Getting out of the camp was easier than she imagined. First, she asked Mrs. Epstein to watch the kids, feigning illness. Then she walked into the woods between where she knew the guards were posted. She'd simply snipped the chain-link fence and slipped out.

She wavered about leaving the note for her parents, unsure of what to say to them. She knew they were coming back at some point later in the day. By her estimation, she would be back before they even got to the HQ. However, just in case, she decided to leave them a quick note so they wouldn't worry. She knew she was right to try to stop Tank. He would only cause her and the entire camp trouble. Stealing a Mason jar full of tack nails and some extra bullets for her rifle, she set out.

Lea hiked almost to the marina. It only took her about an hour to get all the way down the winding roadside to the base of it, near the four-way stop. It was at this stop that one would choose to either take the road up to the camp or head in a different direction. Tracing her steps back toward the camp, she decided on the perfect spot to lay the tacks. She shook out the tacks onto the road, careful to concentrate them where the tires of a car would be.

Once the tacks were in place, she jogged back up the road to the camp. She found a flat, hidden spot to wait. She laid a dirty towel on the ground and then set up her rifle. She tried to remember what the officer at the range had told her about shooting downwind. Something about counting or offsetting the scope, she couldn't recall. The memory was foggy. She mostly used the pistol and wished she had one now instead of this ancient-looking rifle. Oh well. She'd make do. Hopefully, the tacks would stop Tank and she wouldn't need to shoot out his tires.

She waited in her position for what seemed to be an eternity. Boredom quickly set in, making her wonder how long she would have to sit there until he rolled past. She tried to stay alert by counting, doing mental math and other boring things until finally dullness turned to sleepiness. Her head dropped and then jerked back up as she fought sleep. Standing up, she decided to jog in place to get her blood flowing. Once alert again, she settled back into place.

Looking through the rifle scope, she scanned the woods across the street. Trees and more trees blended together in a seamless span of various shades of green. Dullness started to creep back into her mind. She fought it as best as she could. Suddenly, something moved, catching her eye. She focused on the area where she saw movement.

Mom? What the hell?

Her parents were walking on the other side of the road, basically cutting their way through the forest. *Shit. What are they doing here?*

"Mom! Dad! Over here!" she yelled across the road.

Sam and Jane quickly spotted her and ran toward her.

"Lea! Geez! What the hell are you doing out here?" yelled Jane.

Sam grabbed Lea and held her in a tight embrace.

"What do you mean? Didn't you see my note? Tank is out here looking for me. I can't let him get to the camp. He'll wreck everything for the people there and it's all because of me. He just wants me. I have to stop him, Mom!"

Tears streamed down Lea's grimy face as all of her bravery melted under Jane's warm, loving embrace.

"You don't have to do anything alone, baby. We're all in this together. We'll fight Tank head-on, together."

"If anything happened to you, I don't know what we'd do," said Sam, stroking her back.

The three stood in silence as mom and daughter embraced.

"I placed a line of tack nails across the road. I thought I could at least give him a flat. That'd slow him down a little," said Lea.

"That's not a bad idea, honey, but what are you doing here?" asked Sam.

"Well, if the tacks didn't work, then I figured I would shoot out his tires."

"Oh crap. Bad idea. We need to get out of here and back to HQ. The sooner we're behind the fence, the safer we'll all be," said Jane.

"Get down! I hear something!" said Sam urgently.

The three ducked down behind the low brush of the forest just as Tank's Trans Am rolled past them. He was alone, one hand on the steering wheel and the other stretched out the open window.

"Shit! He made it through! We need to warn the camp!" said Lea.

"No! We stay put until he's gone. They can handle him. I'll radio HQ and let them know he's in the area and to be vigilant," said Jane.

After calling HQ, the three waited for a little longer before deciding to start hiking back to the safety of the camp. They all knew eventually Tank would turn around and pass them on his way home. Fear bolstered their alertness as they walked, listening for any sound of his vehicle.

"Did you hear that? I think he's coming," said Jane.

The trail had meandered away from the road and onto a higher elevation. They were able to look down onto the roadway without being seen. The three waited and listened. After a short time, a pickup truck with two hard-looking men drove past their location. On the side of the truck were the words "New Order."

"We're definitely not alone up here. Let's pick up the pace. The chief needs to know that we should move the HQ to Doris's house sooner rather than later before the New Order or Tank finds us all," said Jane.

The family moved through the forest with a quick purposeful step. Their once triumphant, safe world morphed again into something unpredictable.

THE END

THE ADVENTURE WILL CONTINUE WITH BOOK 3 in the FALL of 2017. Sign up for my newsletter below for news about the third book.

Visit **eepurl.com/ctOGAD** to join LEE WEST'S NEWSLETTER for periodic news about Lee West's work and updates about new releases.

You can contact Lee West at leewestbooks@gmail.com

LOOKING FOR ANOTHER HOT POST-APOCALYPTIC SERIES? Check out USA Today bestselling author Steven Konkoly's PERSEID COLLAPSE saga. *Available free through Kindle Unlimited.*

Visit StevenKonkoly.com for more details

About the Author

Lee West is the pen name for a well-known constitutional scholar and liberty advocate. Lee resides in the heart of "fly-over" country, balancing a professional career, with the joys of a hectic family life, two tireless dogs, and a community of friends. Lee particularly enjoys spending time outdoors with family, regardless of the weather! From snowshoeing to kayaking, cross-country skiing to hiking, mountain biking to recreational shooting, Lee brings (drags!) the entire crew along—even if the dogs are the only willing participants.

As a military veteran, Lee has spent countless hours advocating on behalf of veterans for increased benefits, better representation and more equitable treatment by employers and the government. Lee stands proud with the millions of veterans who have sacrificed in the past to preserve liberty at home and abroad—and all of those who carry that torch forward today.

Lee has also spent a significant amount of time working closely with the selfless professionals comprising our justice system—from law enforcement agencies to our courts. *The Blue Lives Apocalypse* series is dedicated to the "men and women in blue," who show up without fail or question.

Lee encourages you to reach out with questions about the series at leewestbooks@gmail.com.

Made in the USA
San Bernardino, CA
18 November 2017